Gracie Rising: The Scars Beneath

An Autobiography by Gracie J

Dedication

This book is dedicated first and foremost to my family. Although we are not always viewing things on the same page, you three mean the world to me and I have never lost sight of the warriors we are.

I also want to dedicate this book to all of the people who helped me along the way, whether they know it or not. To all of the teachers, mentors, colleagues, and friends that were always there for me, this is for you.

Preface

There I sat, 25 years old, and about two weeks away from celebrating my 26th birthday. Christmas was the day before and I was enjoying a movie I had received as a gift. A movie I had watched numerous times growing up, but not a widely known movie. You know- one of those movies that was on television randomly on the weekend evenings between 'Scooby Doo' on Cartoon Network, and 'Are you Afraid of The Dark' on Nickelodeon. I was still amazed that my friend was able to track down the movie considering all I told him pre-Christmas was the basic storyline of a child actor from Jurassic Park starring in it, and the name of the movie was possibly "The Cure". Christmas morning came, and so did the exact movie I was thinking of. I cuddled up to watch the old favorite in my cozy South New Jersey apartment, expecting to feel much excitement as I did when I was a child. I definitely felt a lot of emotions throughout the movie, and as I sat there and reflected on what I was feeling and why (as I often did), I realized how empathetic I had become, and what led to those feelings. I also realized I am not so sure I have ever truly understood all of my emotions, or I should say — where they come from.

And don't worry, I am not just talking about sad emotions, there were happy ones too. When the two young characters (Dexter and Eric) were venturing down the river towards New Orleans, I definitely re-lived the sense of adventure I wanted as a child viewer. I remember sitting on my living room floor, wrapped in a blanket imagining myself making a similar raft to the one the boys were using in the movie, and floating down the river to an unknown destination. Later that summer, my close friends Joey, Dan and I actually attempted to do so. We loaded our backpacks with junk food, bathing suits and man-made fishing poles. We fished along the sides of our wooden pylon "ship" and even caught a large fish that "scared the underwear off of me". We threw it back, of course. We hit some bridges, which eventually cut our trip short.

Aside from that scene, I cannot say there were too many scenes in the movie, which, as a now 25 year-old woman, I did not somehow relate to, or feel some sad or deep emotional connection to.

In the movie, when Eric's mother is physically abusing him, I held back the tears to avoid having flashbacks to my own abuse throughout my childhood. When Dexter's mom is upset as she watches her son's illness progress for the worse, I can feel her sadness and fear as she copes with an illness where outcomes are uncertain. When Eric is experiencing love from another person-- from a source that is not his family, and I can see the confusion in his mind, I related to that exact feeling. When Eric does anything he can to find a cure for his friend's disease, I felt myself re-live my early adolescence as I searched for a cure for my mother's cancer. When Dexter's mom stands up for Eric against Eric's abusive mother, I cried and wished someone did that for me against my brother. And when Dexter passes away at the end, I felt the pain of watching a mother lose her child, and related it to my mother's pain my mother was unable to re-connect with one of her children. This movie, which I had always seen as adventurous and intriguing as a child, was now seen as relatable and deeply emotionally story as an adult to me.

After the movie concluded, I began to reflect on my life again. I did this often, especially after moving out of my home in Connecticut to pursue my dream career. I realized it had been so long since I had been able to express and feel true emotion. Most of my life I was so scared to show any emotions, and at that moment I finally felt that I was free and could let my walls down. I felt alive.

This is when I opened my laptop and decided to get back to writing my story. Not because I want people to know what I went through, but so I could have closure and could feel those feelings freely and not be afraid of my past. I decided I wanted to reach out to those who need to see that no matter what you face in life-- you are in control of what you do in life, and who you become.

You don't have to be a victim just because people view you as a victim; rather you can turn your life around one struggle at a time, and be a hero to yourself. Once you become a hero in your own eyes, you are free to live and be a hero to someone you may not even know you are helping.

My tattoos have become my expression of my life's story. I have always been of the belief that tattoos, being permanent, should have deep and meaningful connection to the individual. All of them I designed at different stages in my life. My inked artwork, as an adult, became my way of talking about my story openly. This is my inked story.

The Gate Tattoo

"C617866, June 28, 1988" and straight lines forming the image of a gate. A tattoo on my inner bicep of my left arm. This is the tattoo representing my adoption. The top of this image reads "C617866" in dots—this being the passport number on my infant passport from India. A passport I did not know existed until my late twenties. I came across it as I cleaned my mother's home in Wallingford, Connecticut one winter, while she was away recovering from an injury. Next is an image of lines, mimicking the only picture I had (at the time) of the iconic gate which stood outside of my orphanage in Calcutta, India. The lines recreate the visible part of that gate shown in a picture I came across online during my research and discussions with other adoptees about the orphanage. "June 28, 1988" in a bold and not so perfect font, replicates the passport stamp of the date I entered the United States of America. I landed in John F. Kennedy Airport at 6 months old, in a basket with another child.

I don't remember too much about my adoption, well at least ever being in India. I was adopted when I was six months old from Calcutta, India. Three pounds, seven ounces is what I weighed when I came home and I was born premature. I will never know my birth weight, or the exact moment I was born. I was thought to have been born in a nursing home in Calcutta and then moved to the orphanage. The International Mission of Hope--an organization that has since been shut down, ran the orphanage. The orphanage had a steel gate at its entrance, with the "IMH" logo within its center.

June 28, 1988. My adoptive mother arrived at the airport along with many other eager parents from the adoption agency, excited to have additions to their families.

My mom has many times told me that, as the babies arrived off the plane, nestled in brown wicker baskets, she frantically searched the name bracelets on all the children dressed in pink. As she went baby-to-baby, basket-to-basket, she checked each bracelet carefully.

She described her feelings of panic to me as she searched and could not find the baby she was waiting for. Frantically, she asked for assistance, and began checking the babies dressed in blue attire. After much exhaustion, finally, my mother had found me. Dressed all in blue with my name band all the way up on shoulder, she picked me up out of my basket.

She placed me on her shoulder and, according to her recollection; I spewed my pacifier across the airport terminal at John F. Kennedy in New York and let out the large wail of a scream into her ear. I still joke with her in saying that should have been an indication of what was to come in the future. I always say she exaggerates that part of the story.

My mother told me that as a young baby, I ate and ate, and well, ate. My mom was a single mother of Italian upbringing. She cooked dinner for us (my brothers, grandfather and I) most nights when she was not working late at the elementary school. Usually we had well- rounded meals with vegetables, meats, and a carbohydrate of some sort. (I was a sucker for her homemade Italian gravy and pasta). If it wasn't a home cooked meal, it was often cheese pizza from Stella's Pizza, a hometown favorite of mine.

I am not sure how my mother ever discovered this habit I had, but I remember being sneaky at the dinner table and her questioning me one night. Sometimes we would eat on paper plates and I would go back for a second serving. Many times, for who knows how many years, I learned to slyly hide that second plate of food upstairs in my bedroom under my bed. I would then, later at night, before bed and after my mother had said goodnight to me, crawl under my bed and consume the left-over food. My mom eventually caught on and had questioned me. Later in life, she credited that to me being malnourished as an infant and feeling like I needed to hoard food in fear of not being fed again. My therapist agreed it may have been related to experiences as an infant starving in India.

The physical affects, like malnourishment, of being born in a third world country, was not the only post-adoption effect that showed in my early childhood. The emotional impact of being adopted into a single parent family and being of another skin color also effected me at an early age. When I was young, I did not understand what adoption was, much like many young children.

I recall one evening, around the age of five, yelling at my mother. It was just after I had finished a warm bath adventure with my many Barbie dolls. Likely Scuba Barbie, whose legs would turn black to represent a wet suit in the warm water. I was getting dried off and avoiding my mom putting the cold moisturizer on my skin. I am unsure what triggered it, but my mother walked out of the room as I began to cry and scream at the top of my lungs. I yelled "you aren't my real mother, and my mother didn't want me". I then began to cry.

Looking back on that night as an adult, I can only imagine the hurt that phrase inflicted on my mother. However, I also know my mother knew I was just a child and did not understand how I came to be where I was at the current time. She came back upstairs after I had settled down and cradled me in her arms. She explained to me that my mother did love me, very much to the point she gave me up for adoption so I could have opportunities and a better life. I never would really understand what she meant until later in life.

Fathers' Day was always tough for me, especially growing up without a father; I did not call anyone "dad". In school when we would make a father's day gift I would always envy the other children and think I was weird because I did not have a dad. Most of my friends would ask me "what do you mean you don't have a dad" and I never knew what to say. I eventually learned to just make a card for my grandfather who lived with my family at our house. This avoided any weird conversations in school. Later in life, as I will explain, the impact of not having a father figure and longing for that connection, emotionally steered my life during young adulthood.

The hardest thing to deal with growing up were the stares. Stares from my friends in school and other children in supermarkets when I was with my mom. I was of Indian descent and my mother was of Italian. We clearly looked different. Numerous times I would be in line with my mother at various locations and would hear a child ask his or her mother, as he/she pointed to me, why I looked different than my mother. I wish I could recall what the responses were as I doubt many parents knew how to explain the situation when caught off guard.

My mother was tuned in and aware of all the "issues" that children and parents alike experience when adopting a child from another country. She ensured my brothers and I attended regular therapy sessions starting at a young age. When I would go to see my therapist-- Terry was her name-- I would usually play with toys in a room, on the soft carpet while Terry would ask me questions. Most of the time I did not know why Terry was asking about my mom and family, and how I was feeling but I liked Terry and she was always nice to me. I trusted her and it seemed as though she was able to explain the whole adoption phenomenon to me quite well. She would observe me, and write notes down on her notepad and I, many times thought she was just drawing pictures. I soon learned that I wasn't different than any other child. My family just wasn't the all American family, with a mom, dad, kids and a dog, all of the same race. And that was okay.

"Wallyworld"

The state of California wrapped around my left rib cage with an image of the late Hartford Whalers National Hockey League logo placed in southern California. California being a representation of achieving my bucket-list item of driving across country to LA at age 24 and the Hartford Whalers representing my love for my home state and the beloved late NHL hockey team.

I grew up in a small town in the Connecticut suburbs called Wallingford or sometimes called "Wallyworld" by most of the locals. Wallingford is situated in central Connecticut, between the interstate 91 corridor and Route 15, also known as the Merritt Parkway. The town has two high schools- Lyman Hall High School on the east side and Sheehan High School on the west side. A small-town feel but not too small. Everyone knows each other from local school events or fundraisers. The town has been run by one mayor, Mayor William Dickenson for over 30 years and has a good combination of rolling farm hills in contrast with the local businesses in the downtown area. Some good local spots include Gouveia Vineyards along the Connecticut Wine Trail, Rosa's Deli on Route 5, and Archie Moore's on North Main Street. All spots I still frequent whenever I am home. It's also the town with the zip code 06492 used in the television show, the Gilmore Girls. I grew up on a dead end street, at the bottom of Ward Street Extension.

My street once had a walking bridge that connected Backes Court to Dolittle Park. In the summers, our street would always be packed with people who would park on our street to walk down the bridge to the baseball diamond. A hurricane took the bridge out in the mid 1990's and it was never rebuilt, but as a teenager it was still popular hang out spot for my friends and I.

My childhood friend Joey and I would always head down to the bridge, hot dogs and bread in hand to catch the latest fish down at the river. We both sometimes needed that escape from our families. It became one of my fondest summer memories as a child.

To this day Joey and I still remember the journey down the bank of the river to relax and get away from the madness we were experiencing at home. Joey was like a brother to me, and to this day I am grateful he is in my life.

I had two best girl friends I grew up with, Maria and Ava. Both lived across the street from me and we still know each other to this day. Many summer days were spent making mud piles, "gunk" chalk, arguing over who was better-N'SYNC or Backstreet boys and then singing those songs and putting on "concerts" for our neighbors in our front yards. Ava and I started a dog treat business when I was in middle school where we combined peanut butter and dog treats, baked them in our ovens and walked around our neighborhood selling them. Ava, Maria and I also sold lemonade (which was actually Crystal Lite) at the end of the street during the summer in my little red radio flyer wagon. The summers were full of bike rides and swimming in Maria's pool.

When the summer would come to an end, we would prepare for that classic first day of school picture and the ridiculous embarrassment by our parents as we got older and wanted to walk to the bus alone. As the fall came, the three of us would pile leaves high and jump into them as we bagged the leaves into the trash bags that looked like jack-0-lanterns. We would begin to decorate our houses like a haunted house, with spider webs, and tombstones. Maria and her dad grew giant pumpkins in their yard and one year, her dad grew a pumpkin large enough for us to fit in. Apple picking was also a staple of the fall. Mom would take us to Lyman Orchards in Middlefield, CT as soon as the apples were in season. We would bake apple pies and make applesauce from the hand picked apples. Fall was, and still is my favorite season.

In the winters we would build igloos and forts in the snow pile that was at the end of the street. We would use food coloring and water to spray color on the snow. Many time my brothers would come out and we would build snow bunkers in the front yard and have snowball fights until the sun went down. The winters were cold, and I would stand on the back deck and strip all my wet clothes off down to my long johns as my mother would hand me a warm cup of hot chocolate until I had all the layers off. It always reminded me of that scene from A Christmas Story, where Ralphie's brother couldn't put his arms down because of all his layers. My mother always wanted us bundled up.

The spring was full of flowers and allergies. Oh and I mean allergies! I am convinced that to this day, I suffer from horrible spring allergies as a result of my genetics, and not being used to the types of pollen in the United States. I would always feel sick for a month. The spring also meant Easter egg hunts at Dolittle Park and warm weather. I loved when it started to get warm-It meant more time to be outside after school. It also meant that school was almost out for summer break.

Other than the season changes which were always memorable in New England, my mom was an elementary school teacher in the town over-Northford Public Schools. So during the school year, none of my brothers and I could do much wrong without her knowing. I remember being in the first grade and stapling my finger multiple times with a small stapler. A stapler I wasn't supposed to have and got at a teacher's store with my mom the previous weekend. She found out and by the time I got home, I was already in trouble.

Growing up in Wallingford was full of memories- both good and bad. I grew up in the same home my entire life (minus a few years we will talk about later) and on the same street. My mother chose Wallingford, specifically the east side, because of the diversity to help my brothers and I feel more comfortable. I still go home a lot to see my friends from childhood, and as much as I love frequenting the local spots and being around my friends, I am rarely in that childhood home I grew up in. Why? My therapists explained it to me as having Post Traumatic Stress Disorder, commonly known as PTSD from what took place in my home as a child. I limit my time home to seeing my mother and making sure she knows I love her, playing with my puppy who is like my child, and then being with my friends out of my house. This helps me avoid the anxious feelings I constantly feel when at home. My friends have always been my rocks in life, and at many times throughout my childhood, they were my protectors and my family when I felt as if my family had abandoned me. In my eyes, my childhood ended at age 10. I do not have any memories that are positive, from my childhood after age 10, in that home in Wallingford I used to love.

The Happy Moments

I have two brothers I grew up with: Ethan and Noah. Well really only one (another story for later). Noah was 3 years older than I --and Ethan was three years older than Noah. This made me the youngest of the bunch. All three of us were adopted from India as infants from orphanages. All three adopted by a single mother who wanted to love the big brown eyed, dark skinned Indian babies and give us a new opportunity in the United States. Ethan was the darker complexion of the three of us and being the first one to come home, he was the only one to really live outside of Wallingford, Connecticut. According to my mother, Ethan got bullied a bit more for his darker skin complexion when he was young. This was part of the reasoning for my mother moving the family to Wallingford before I came home.

Growing up until age 10, I was closest to Noah. Being that Noah and I were closer in age, we tended to be around each other a lot. Noah and I would spend the summers playing basketball and rollerblading on the dead end street. I played the flute for the school band and Noah played the drums. I always thought it was so cool Noah was a drummer and I looked up to him a lot as a musician.

Ethan, Noah and I would interact in the summers mostly when it began to get hot. We did not have a pool so our relief came in the form of Super Soaker fights. We would save the allowance from chores our mother would give us and hopefully buy the best Super Soaker there was, to dominate each other come summertime. Ethan, by far, had the best one. Ethan had the Super Soaker that was like the BB Gun in A Christmas story. I remember it well- it had 3 water storage tanks on a backpack, connected to a multi-function nozzle to spray water at numerous levels at the opponents. Noah and I had the classic one bottle green pump Super Soakers. The key was to gain control over the water hose in the backyard. Usually Ethan won that and would have that endless access to the water supply.

Vacations at a young age were also another one of the few memories I have with my family all together. My mother would take my brothers and I up north to New Hampshire to visit our cousins. The trips were in "Big Red" which was mom's big red Chevrolet van, equipped with 2 bench seats and full backseats. Mom would pack us all a zip-lock bag of snacks and a backpack with miscellaneous games and toys to keep us occupied for the car ride. If we didn't fall asleep on the drive, we were usually picking on each other. I remember one time Ethan telling me Barney the dinosaur was on the side of the road and I went crazy looking for him and he wasn't there.

The trip down to Virginia Beach was the longest trip I can remember. We were in the van and when we were on the Chesapeake Bay bridge, which was two lanes at the time, whenever a large truck would pass us, my mother would tell us how she "white knuckled" the steering wheel as the van would shift as the truck passed on the other side. I also remember being out on a whale watch and my hat blowing away and being super upset about losing that hat.

Southington, Connecticut was another spot of fun summer memories for all of us. Mom would pack the blankets into the car, make homemade, stove-top popcorn and we would jump into the van to head to the drive-in movie theater. She would pull up in 'big-red' and we would open the back of the van and set up the blankets and have the old metal microphone tuned to the correct radio station. I remember watching "The Goonies" and "Hook" at the drive-in. it always amazed me how they got the picture onto the big screen. Summers were also full of strawberry picking at the local farms.

I am not sure why these memories stick out, but they are the happy memories I have of our little family. It was when I was ten years old when our little family would be torn upside down.

The Diagnosis

It was President's day weekend, 1998. I just turned 10 years old. My mom hadn't been feeling well for a month or so. She was having trouble going up and down the stairs at home and was always tired, much more than usual. She asked me to go to see the doctor with her at the Mid-State Walk In clinic. I did not have much choice and hopped in the car and off we went. We saw Doctor Martha. A beautiful middle-aged blonde woman, tall and extremely articulate. She sat there and listened intently as my mother described her symptoms to her. I always hated when doctors did not seem to listen to your symptoms but you could tell Dr. Martha was different. What seemed as if it could have just been a run of the mill winter virus, Dr. Martha still wanted to check all of the boxes. She checked my mom's lymph notes and temperature, made sure she didn't have strep and then sent her for some blood work in the end. We went on our way. The long weekend went by and the blood work results came back.

I can only retell this part based on what my mom told me when I got older, on how she got the news. My mom was at work when Dr. Martha called her. Dr. Martha asked her to come in as soon as she could. My mom- being the stubborn Italian that she was, refused to wait and requested numerous times to be told over the phone. Dr. Martha respected the request and told her. "Linda, you have Acute Lymphocytic Leukemia. Your white blood cell count is in the thousands and your red blood cell count is one. You are extremely ill and need to be admitted to the hospital as soon as possible." I cannot begin to imagine what went through my mom's head at this very moment, but being an adult now, I can imagine the pain and fear. She was a single parent, with no close family and had less than 24 hours to figure out what to do. On top of that, she had to accept she had a life threatening disease. My mom told me the doctor's did not think she would live.

That night I got off the school bus and walked down the street. I remember walking up to the house and seeing Helen, my mother's close friend, outside of the house.

My mother told me to go across the street to Maria's and she would see me there shortly. I was in Maria's bedroom playing music when Deanne, Maria's mom came in and asked me to come into the living room. She asked Maria to stay in the bedroom. I came out into the living room. My mom was sitting there, and she didn't seem herself. Her cheery red face and big smile were not there. I sat next to her on the couch and she turned to me.

"Gracie remember when mommy went to the doctor's last week?" she said to me.

"Yes" I replied.

"Well, I am very sick and I need to go away for a while to get better. You are going to stay with Aunt Ro in North Haven while I get better."

"OK." I reply, not understanding the depth of the situation.

"We are going to go back home and I need you to pack some clothes for a while." We left Deanne's and walked across the street.

I walked across the street, and up into the house. Helen was there. I walked into my bedroom, and there was a brand new blue and pink duffle bag with wheels on my bed. I saw my brothers had already packed and had new bags as well. I began to pack my favorite clothes, a few books, my Spice Girl CD and my Aladdin soundtrack. My mom joined me and made sure I had everything I needed. Later that night, Helen brought Noah and I to North Haven where our aunt lived. I later found out that Ethan, given his age and where his high school was located, was able to stay at home so he could get to school. My mom said her good byes to us, and to this day I have no idea how she stayed so strong and didn't cry.

I was in the third grade, and my teacher was Mrs. Monica Aurora at Evarts C. Stevens. Noah was in the fifth grade at the same school. During the week, my mom's close friends Paula and Scott, along with Mrs. Aurora would pick Noah and I up from my aunt's in North Haven during the week and bring us to school in Wallingford. Scott had a small puppy named Lucky, a white little fluff ball that I loved to ride in the car with. They always made me smile when they picked me up. Frankly, I think Noah and I enjoyed the break from our Aunt's very regimented schedule at home.

At this point I want to take the time to thank my teachers. Teachers were always prominent in my life given my mother being a teacher. My brothers and I grew up spending summers in our mother's classroom helping her prepare it for the fall school year. We came to know her co-workers as family. We were always around teachers and felt comfortable around them. They became even more important to me as time went on.

During this time, Mrs. Aurora was my hero. She had no idea what was going on fully, but knew at the surface my mother was sick. For me, seeing her pull up in the morning, I can still remember the excited feeling of getting to take a ride to school with MY teacher. Her soft voice, enthusiastic attitude and warm hug when she saw me made me feel safe. Safe at a time where I felt alone, scared, and out of place. To Monica- thank you. To Mrs. Wollen- the gym teacher. Gym was my favorite place during the school day, along with most other students. Mrs. Wollen was a young teacher, new to our school, but full of smiles and so kind. She would always compliment me and give me a high five after class. Although I am sure she did it to every student, I always felt she believed in me. And at this time I never thought anyone believed in me. So thank you Mrs. Wollen for being that person.

Our aunt was very strict on rules, bed time and house etiquette. We watched very little television. Noah and I usually stayed outside to keep ourselves occupied. We had household chores and always made sure to complete them all. We would go to church on Sundays and prayed before bed every night. I would usually end the night writing in my diary about whatever the day had in store and listening to the Aladdin soundtrack, particularly the song- "A Whole New World". I remembered singing to that song and praying for my mother to come back soon.

That spring flew by and there wasn't too much I really remember from it. I had braces and would continue to see my orthodontist in Wallingford, attending school in Wallingford and missing my friends back home. I missed my mom, but I felt like I was on a temporary vacation. The summer began and halfway through, I remember going to visit my mom for the first time.

Helen picked us all up, and Noah, Ethan and I were taken to the Hospital of Saint Raphael in New Haven, Connecticut. I believe my mom was on the "Solantano Floor" most of her stay during her illness, but when we went to visit her she was just getting moved out of the Intensive Care Unit. Seeing her for the first time was something I will never forget.

We walked onto the hospital floor, and we had to wear booties on our feet to enter the room. I walked into the room, looked at the bed and saw a woman I didn't recognize. I saw the eyes and smile that I knew, but her hair had all fallen out. She wore a mask around her face. She had lost a large amount of weight, and her energy was low. Her hands were cold. She cried as we walked into the room. She was hooked up to a bunch of machines and had tubes coming out of her. She had what was called a port in her chest and the room smelled like plastic. We couldn't stay long, but I remember not knowing what I was feeling. I stood there, confused and just hugged Helen as we walked out, not knowing when I would see my mom again.

The summer was coming to an end, and it was becoming too much for our elderly aunt to care for us. The new school year would be starting soon, and it was decided that Noah, Ethan and I would need to live somewhere else and switch schools. So we did just that. Left our teachers and friends behind, and moved to New Haven, CT.

Tzdek & Cold Spring Street

It's pronounced "Tzdek" in Hebrew, loosely meaning Justice and Righteousness. Written in Hebrew inside my right wrist. The hand you take an oath with. I learned Hebrew while living away from my mother during the time she was hospitalized when I attended Hebrew School in New Haven, Connecticut. I got this tattoo in 2011, to represent my graduation from a training academy for my dream job. I first saw this scripture written at the Holocaust Museum in Washington, DC. For me it represents the oath I took to protect this country, and to symbolize freedom and karma. Those who do bad will get what they deserve in life, I just need to do good and not retaliate for the hurt I have felt due to others' actions.

The same day I found my baby passport from India, I also came across documents my mother had written related to the time she was in the hospital and who was to care for us while she was sick. I remember shuffling through some papers and reading "To whom it may concern" across the top. I stopped and thought to myself… "Do I want to read on? Do I want to re-live this painful time?" I read on. Here is where when I can say, tears came to my eyes. My mother agreed to pay the woman who cared for us during her hospitalization $1500.00 a month. I sat down after reading this. Not because of the amount, although it was a lot. But because my mother to this day doesn't know what went on in the household she placed us in. She thought this "family friend" would care for us as if we were her own. I did not even know where to start when I had to decide whether or not to write about the experience at this temporary home. A home of a woman I had grown up knowing and playing in the park with her children. Children whom she too adopted from other countries. A woman my mother trusted and saw as a trusted friend. A woman who, looking back now, in my eyes, who never deserved the friendship of my mother.

I do not know if my mom is going to read this book, or this chapter. And for that- mom I apologize. I apologize for never truly telling you what happened to us while we were there. Partly because I think the three of us (Ethan, Noah and I) blocked a lot of it out. For me- I did not want you to know. Once I was able to process all of what DID happen to us in that woman's house, over a decade later, I decided to never tell you. There was no sense on hurting you more than you were at the end of this situation. So mom- I am sorry. This is the best way for me to have the closure to that part of my life, and I hope you truly understand that I do not hold the choice of you placing us in this home against you at all. You did what you thought was best and had no idea what was going to happen. So what happened? I refer to this time as the "last childhood" part of my life.

1998. Red House. A spiral wooden staircase. The smell of old wood, basement cement, sand, dog hair, and the sound of children. New Haven, Connecticut. This is the house that robbed me of my childhood.

Out of respect I have for people's privacy, I have changed her name in this story. Although I don't think she deserves any bit of respect from my family or I, I will give her the anonymity. So for that purpose I will call her 'Barbara'.

Barbara knew my mother for years before my brothers and I went to live with her. My mother and Barbara met through adoption events in the Connecticut area. I remember meeting her children and playing with them at East Rock park in the summers preceding living with her. She had a son around Noah's age and a daughter closer to mine as well as an infant daughter, whom she recently adopted when we moved in that summer. Barbara ran a daycare during the day at the house for work.

After reading the letter I had stumbled across, I now knew my mother and Barbara in writing, had an agreement that Barbara would care for Ethan, Noah and I and she would be compensated financially while my mother was hospitalized. The agreement also stated it was last only until my mother was able to resume caring for us. We arrived in the late summer of 1998.

I was given a room in the middle floor of the house near her oldest daughter's room, Noah was given the attic room and Ethan (who moved in later during the school year) got a room in the basement.

Noah and I attended the same school-- Worthington Hooker Elementary School. The grades at Worthington Hooker were Kindergarten through 6th grade at the time. Ethan would get up very early and catch a bus in New Haven to go to Wilcox Technical High School, in Meriden, Connecticut.

During the first 6 weeks living at Barbara's, I remember life being "OK". I would go to school, come home, do my homework, and ask Barbara if I could call my mother to say hello. I would walk to and from school everyday. I sometimes would get picked up for therapy or orthodontist appointments by Helen, in the evenings. That was pretty much it. I was allowed to call my mom when Barbara would be done with work. And on weekends, if OK, she would take my brothers and I to see her at the hospital. Things were different and it was a hard adjustment, at least for me. I missed my friends and school back home a lot. And I really missed my mom. I wish this was how my life stayed the remainder of the time at Barbara's, but in the fall, things began to change. Before I go on, I want you to remember, this is ME telling you MY story from my perspective based on what I saw and observed or what I have learned after the fact. I have spoken to my brothers about their recollections in a few conversations, and we all had different perspectives. This is my account of my experience with the observations I saw as a ten year old.

In the fall, Barbara began to ask me to help with the daycare activities. My daily routine began in the morning with preparing medicine and breakfast for the kids before I went to school. I would go to school, and come home. After school I was told to help with the children around the daycare until they were all picked up. I then was tasked with cleaning up the playroom area, which included a sandbox. I still cannot forget the smell and sound of that green sand box as it scraped across the wooden porch every time I had to move it to clean up the excess sand. Barbara began to cut down on the time I was allowed to speak to my mother on the phone. According to Barbara, my mother was too ill to speak on the phone. Eventually, my mornings got even earlier-- around 5am, Barbara would ask me to go get the newspaper on the corner of East Rock State Park. Mind you, I was ten years old, a girl, alone, and East Rock was a large park with a pretty poor safety rating in the late nineties. My mother rarely let me go around the block alone in Wallingford let alone if she knew I was walking to East Rock at 5am alone.

I would make my lunch in the morning, usually a sandwich and juice box, hopefully a pudding if I was lucky or a Jell-O snack. Dinner was never good. I missed my mother's home cooked meals almost immediately. We would eat fish sticks, potato pancakes, macaroni and cheese or any frozen dinner that would suffice. Most nights I wouldn't eat. I hated when Barbara forced me to eat the potato pancakes, and to this day I hate potato pancakes and fish sticks. I gave the dog in the house a lot of my dinner just so I could be excused.

After dinner, I would go upstairs to my room and listen to music. Spice Girls and a song by LeAnn Womack "Hope You Dance" as well as the Little Mermaid Soundtrack. I would put the music on and lock myself into my own little world. I found a black composition notebook around age 20, where I wrote down all my thoughts about what was happening in my life during this time. It's where my idea for this book came in. I read about all of these experiences in this notebook.

When I read the notebook, I began to recount all that had happened to my family and I during this time. Processing this as an adult was much different than as I saw everything as a child. From my notebook, my small chapters with only words known to a ten year old translated to much more as an adult. Some of the experiences I am still not ready to share out to the public, as it still hurts me to think it happened to me, but I am ready to share a few.

My mother's 49th birthday I will never forget. She was born in early September and I wanted to throw her a surprise party with all of her friends to make her smile. I asked Barbara if I could and she agreed. I reached out to her close friends and learned, based on their responses to my invite, my mother was losing friends left and right. This included friends she had for most of her life. In the end, I did not understand why we couldn't have the party but Barbara eventually put a stop to the idea. Years later I found out from my mother, that Barbara was telling my mother's friends a lot of lies about my mother while she was sick. Lies about my mother being an unfit parent, who should not have kids. Barbara killed my mother's soul by saying such horrible things about her. Barbara painted a picture of my mother as a cruel woman who left her kids and was abusive. Barbara made allegations to her friends that she was an unfit parent. My mother talked about these comments years later and I was in shock.

Barbara filed a false claim with the Department of Children and Families (DCF) against my mother, which, over 15 years later, prevented my mother getting a job in childcare once she retired from teaching. My heart broke for her when my mother called me and told me about this filing. I read it and at the time that Barbara was referring to and filed the false claim, my mother was not abusive. She may have disciplined us but she was not an unfit mother. The DCF complaint was never substantiated. If it had been, there is no way we would have been allowed to be back into her care.

Christmas of 1998. That's a story I remember. Noah and I would sneak away sometimes at night into a hideaway that was near Barbara's room. In this little hideaway we would just talk and hang out together. Much like the hideaway you saw the character Harry Potter live in, in "The Sorcerer's Stone." We did this because Barbara kept Noah, Ethan and I all separated from each other and would monitor our interactions.

A few weeks before Christmas, as we prepared the house for Chanukah, Noah and I snuck into the hidden cubby and to our surprise there were three large black trash bags inside the cubby. Being the curious children we were, we opened each bag. We gasped and smiled with excitement when we opened each bag. Inside were gifts wrapped in fun Christmas paper with each of our names on it, "Noah", "Ethan" and "Gracie." Noah and I had long mastered unwrapping gifts and re-wrapping gifts without notice, so we did just that. Inside we found Pokémon cards, Tomagachis, CD players, CDs and other miscellaneous toys that were popular in the late nineties. We ended that night pretty quickly and decided to keep the excitement for Christmas. Barbara allowed us to celebrate both Chanukah and Christmas.

Christmas day rolled along and just as if we were at home, we came running down the stairs eager to see what Santa had brought us. I remember thinking about all of the toys we had seen in the bags and knowing we had the hit the jackpot of toys. Coming downstairs to where the tree was a moment I can't forget. There were a few small boxes. That's it. And I've never been a materialistic child or adult, but I certainly was wondering where all the toys went in the black bags. Being the young naïve child I was, I asked Barbara about their whereabouts and was quickly scolded. I dropped that topic quickly and enjoyed the toys I had received. Fast forward to a few years later--I learned those toys were donated by people from my hometown-- via the Make-A-Wish foundation. The group had heard about my mother's illness and taken up a drive. To this day, I have not discovered where those toys went, and I have shared it with my closest friends. All in all, a person's true colors showed that day to me.

When my mother was released from the hospital and allowed to go home, my brothers and I at least got to talk to her more regularly on the phone. She told me she was trying to get the house ready for us to come home to. She never told me until I was older, how many times and how long she fought to get us back from Barbara's custody that winter. I never truly understood until I found a letter in my mother's belongings years later, addressed to the courts, where my mother requested to have us released from Barbara. I asked my mother about it and she told me it was written because Barbara refused to let us come home to my mother that winter. Barbara was filing false complaints with DCF at the time, which slowed my mother's ability of getting us home.

The best day I ever had in that red house was the last day I was there. Noah and I pulled up in Barbara's Gray mini-van and got out of the car. As we exited, a man in a blue New Haven Police Department uniform said "Are you Noah and Gracie?" I stared at Noah, looked at Barbara and we both went inside the house. Barbara gave us a cautious glare which implied "do not say anything." Barbara didn't want us to answer. I peered around the corner and saw my mother standing outside the house with the officer and her car. I did not want to get in trouble and I thought I was in trouble. After a lengthy back and forth between the officer and Barbara, I remember hearing the man's voice say "Gracie and Noah please come downstairs." We both came down the back stairwell and he told us to pack as much as we could in our bags and to come back down. He told us we were going home with our mother. I had never been so happy in my life and I remember feeling so relieved. Noah had the opposite reaction. We both did as told and around midnight that night we were with mom on the way to Wallingford. Ethan was locked up with the police because Barbara filed a false report on him. My mom went and got him later that night.

I won't get into the details of what else happened in the house as my mother to this day does not know, and I don't want her to know. There is no point in my eyes as an adult to hurt her anymore than she has been already by this woman. My mom did what she needed to and would have never intentionally put us into this bad situation had she known. School was my escape and how I dealt with everything I went through. It was where I felt safe. The song "Concrete Angel" by Martina McBride became a staple on my mixed CD when I walked to school. Music was my way of expressing how I felt. To this day, lyrics and music usually express how I am feeling. The verse "The teacher wonders but she doesn't ask, it's hard to see the pain behind the mask, bearing the burden of a secret storm, sometimes she wishes she was never born."--- That's the verse that was the best way for me to describe how I felt from age 9 until my young adulthood. I learned to hide how I felt, in fear of repercussions when I would get home to Barbara's and then eventually my house in Wallingford.

I celebrated one birthday at Barbara's, and I am glad I never celebrated another there. Although it wasn't a long amount of time, the time at Barbara's did irreversible damage to my family.

Barbara broke my mother's spirit, and tarnished friendships she had made for years. Barbara separated three siblings, treated all three of us differently, and caused us all to lose the bonds we had as children and to lose trust in each other and our mother. Barbara did not show kindness in my eyes or Ethan's, but in the eyes of Noah, she did. The time at Barbara's house was the catalyst that caused my family to fall apart. Eventually I chose to forgive Barbara for her actions as an adult. But the pain and hurt she caused me at a young age-- that took years to overcome.

Hope & Noah

On the back of my neck, in Chinese it reads "Hope" (Don't worry I had my Chinese speaking friend verify this as it was my first tattoo). Below "Hope" it reads "NOAH".

Coming home to Wallingford, CT that first night back from Barbara's was eerie. It was late at night, and we were all exhausted. I walked into the house I had known, and didn't recognize a thing. The house was completely renovated--- new carpets, beds, paint, cleaned top to bottom, new televisions, furniture and the house even smelled new. There was a welcome home sign in the dining room. Noah and I walked in. I hugged mom and went to my room, excited for the new bed. Noah stormed off. I can't remember Ethan's reaction. But we were all home. That's all that mattered. Coming home was different because our Grandpa had been moved to a nursing home as well. He had cancer and Alzheimer's and wasn't living there anymore. The house was just…. different.

The next morning I remember waking up and walking downstairs. I sat down at the dining room table and was wondering what was for breakfast. Mom told me we were going to our favorite place, BICKFORD'S!!!! It was a small pancake house on Route 5 in our town. I was excited and ran upstairs to tell my brothers. They were not nearly as excited as I was.

We ended up going, regardless of their lack-luster response. This is where as a ten year old, I realized the change in my family. We sat there, and it was just a quiet breakfast. My mother did her classic "worm" trick where she would take the wrapper off the straw and keep it super bunched up and then drop a few droplets of water on the paper and watch it grow like a worm. Before she got sick she would always do that with my brother's and they would have a competition of whose worm was better. This time, it seemed as if I was the only one entertained by the old trick. We ordered our pancakes. I don't even remember if we really talked. I think my mom tried to speak to us but all three of us were pretty quiet. Especially Ethan. He seemed to isolate himself. Noah appeared angry and I just wanted pancakes. I did not understand why things felt so different.

Monday came quickly. We headed back to our schools in Wallingford. I went go back to E.C. Steven's and was lucky to have one of my favorite teachers for the remainder of fourth grade. I walked in and all my old classmates had made a Welcome Back sign and signed it. I was so happy to be home and back with my friends. It finally felt like things were normal. Noah went into Dag for middle school. Ethan continued high school at the trade school and was working on getting his learner's permit. Everything seemed to be going well, or so I thought; that's what happens when you're ten and the world is manipulating people around you, and you don't know it. You see life as you should, as a child. I don't think after the day Noah hit me, I ever felt like a child again. I lost my best friend that day. And my family began to fall apart all over again.

"Gracie and Noah let's go, we have to bring Ethan to work" mom yelled to us from the bottom of the stairs. "Mom I want to go to my friend Colin's house" Noah replied. "You can go when we get back, you can stay home if you want" mom yelled back. "Let's go Gracie" she said. "Mom, can't I just stay here with Noah?? I'll be good and do my homework I promise" I said. "Okay, don't leave the house" she agreed. A few minutes later, the car door shut to the blue Impala and they were on their way to New Haven.

I guess it's a good thing I don't remember exactly how I was attacked at first. I remember the hitting, the slamming against the wall, me trying to run to the back door and then being pulled back. I remember screaming and crying and pleading with Noah as he hit me. I remember the pillow on my head on the couch. And I remember finally getting away from him and out of the back door. I ran to my neighbors, Jack and Ann.

Jack and Ann were like my surrogate grandparents and were home more than my mother was during the weekdays. They are two people who I am grateful for in my life for they were always there for me and always saw what was really going on at my house when I felt like no one knew, especially after this day. This day was just the beginning of many worse experiences Jack and Ann would help me through.

They called 911. I was so scared he (Noah) was going to come and get me. He didn't. I just sat there with Jack and Ann, and cried. My mom pulled up just before the ambulance did. The police were already there.

Noah had locked himself in his room and come to find out, he had punched holes into the new walls, in the room that would one day be mine as an adult. He was taken by ambulance to Middletown for a psychological evaluation. I was checked out at the hospital, and then went directly to see my therapist. I remembered not talking much, just saying I was doing my homework and didn't say a word- he just snapped. That was the last time I saw Noah at home with me, as my brother. He was evaluated and released to the custody of the state. My best friend growing up was gone. And it was my fault. That's how I looked at it until I was in my mid twenties.

Noah was put into a foster home in Milford, Connecticut. He switched schools and lived with his new family. He only let my mother and I visit once. We both wrote him letters weekly. Ethan never wanted to visit Noah or expressed interest in contacting him. I'll never forget the last time I saw him regularly during that part of my life. It was January 11th and my 13th birthday. We both had to go to the courthouse to get our naturalizations finalized. I was so happy to see him since I hadn't seen or talked to him in years at this point. I figured he knew it was my 13th birthday since we had always been so close growing up. I expected a hug and a happy birthday. I got nothing, no hug, no happy birthday just a nod at the courthouse. I don't even remember what I had to do for the naturalization process that day besides sign my certificate with my full name, including my Indian name. I was so upset. I got in the car, and I couldn't cry, I just remember thinking about how much he hated me and that I deserved it. I had taken his life and family away from him. I shouldn't have run from the house that day. That's what I was thinking. Watching my mother being so upset that her son didn't talk to her. Come to find out a few weeks later, Noah requested to have her parental rights terminated. My mother agreed to it after years of trying to get him to talk to her and believing that was the only thing that would make him happy.

My mother slipped into a depression that I can't fully describe. She tried to stay happy, celebrate holidays during the first year or two that Noah was gone. But that eventually faded away. We stopped celebrating holidays as a family and eating meals at the table. She would lock herself in the computer room at night or lay on the couch and watch television after work. It was like she was a zombie with nothing to live for. She looked empty. She had no light in her eyes. Once Noah severed her parental rights, my mother was no more. She was not allowed to contact him. He would not contact her. She and I did not know where he was or if he was alive. As time went on, we knew he was not at the foster home anymore. He had left when he was able to and no one knew where he had gone. When I would see the friends he used to talk to around Wallingford, I would ask them if they had talked to or seen Noah. Unfortunately, I did not have any success with that method. My mother was an amazing person who adopted three children as a single parent, battled cancer, won, and now her light was gone.

I never really truly understood what she was feeling during her depression until I began to battle with depression myself.

Then There Were 2

As my mother slipped into a deep depression, I don't remember her being much of a presence in my life. She would bring me to school occasionally, but most days I would just rollerblade with my friends Joey and Dan to middle school and then stay after school for sports. My friend Joey was my hero as a kid. We made a connection when we were young over something I would never wish on any child. He understood what I was going through at home. With my mother being gone most hours at the elementary school, and usually there later in the evening prepping for the next day or conferences, I was usually home with my brother Ethan. I think my mother consumed herself with her students and worked to mask the pain she was in, and when she would come home to a home without Noah, she was numb inside. Ethan had his own demons. And this is what Joey understood and I cannot thank him enough for being there for me.

As the time went on without Noah in the house, Ethan became outwardly angrier. He and I had no friendship or brother / sister relationship. I rarely interacted with him and we were quite the opposite of each other. I was 6 years younger and very outgoing. I was an athlete and becoming known in the town for being good at track and basketball. He went to a different school, in a different town and was very introverted. Most people did not even know he was my brother. Joey and I had similar home lives in that sense—we both never wanted to go home. We knew if we did, we might say something wrong, or just do something wrong and it would end with a physical fight with our older sibling. And that's what it was. I think Ethan had a lot of built up anger and things that I could not understand, but I had to try to understand as an adult, in order to forgive him. He did not have a father figure, he was bullied when he was young, he was different in appearance and we both lost our mother, in a sense, at times in our lives when we needed her. He was alone, and I think he bottled his anger up and took it out on me. I was an easy target and probably an annoying little sister at times. But it wasn't the physical abuse weekly that really got to me.

I grew up thinking that was "normal." It was the emotional abuse. That has been the lasting effect on me and took me well over 10 years to understand, and work through. From around the time Noah left when I was in 4th grade, to the end of high school, I cannot remember having a day where I was not scared of Ethan, or felt like my mother was completely absent emotionally from my life, allowing Ethan to act the way he did.

Ethan would call me names like "Maggot." He would make fun of my buck teeth, my smile, my overbite, and my headgear. He would tease me about how I looked and tell me that I was ugly. He would scream at me at the top of his lungs, inches from my face, terrifying me. He would tower over me and remind me that I was the reason that Noah left and that mom got sick. He would remind me that I was nothing and meant nothing to anyone. These words, over and over for 10 years. They scarred me. Learning to forgive Ethan was one of the hardest challenges of my adult life. From age 9 until I was around 21 years old, Ethan would remind me that everything that was wrong with our family was MY fault and every thing about me was a failure. That was what I remember from growing up after Noah was gone.

No family time. No holidays. Constantly trying to hide the pain on my face at school and avoid going home. Never feeling loved or good enough. Always feeling ugly. Feeling ashamed of who I was and feeling alone. That is all I remember. And it was all I believed. School was my safe place.

An Unexpected Visitor

I was in the 7th grade, in Earth Science class. Someone called the classroom telephone and my teacher told me to report downstairs to the office. I thought I was in trouble. I walked down to the office and, to my surprise, Noah was standing there. I remember hugging him and smiling. He stated he was not supposed to be there but he told me he wanted to apologize to me for what he had done. He also told me not to tell my mother he had visited. The visit was not more than five minutes long. To this day, I still can't remember if I even said anything. I am sure I did, hopefully that I missed him and loved him. But I was in shock to see my brother, and I know I wish he would just come home.

I went back to class and I remember sitting in the back of the classroom, and my eyes filled with tears. The class period was coming to an end, and as the bell rang to switch classes, we all stood up. The tears dripped slowly down my cheeks, and my teacher pulled me aside. I tried to spit out the words that my brother had visited me, but I knew it would make no sense to her as to why that would have upset me. She took me down to the guidance office. This would be the first time in my life that someone in the school system would see the internal struggles I was having. But even then, I was already so used to locking my feelings up, that I still masked a lot of my pain. Talking about Noah was easy because he was my friend and I missed him dearly, but speaking out about what Ethan did to me, that wouldn't happen. I was scared Ethan would somehow find out. I also was so used to the things that were said to me and did not know any better that I did not think they were things I needed to talk about. I did not know they were wrong. So at that time in my life, no one would know about those interactions, which shaped the rest of my teenage years. They just knew about Noah being gone.

At this time, I still did not make it known to any of my teachers what was going on at home. I did not know anything was "wrong" at home because that is all I knew. My mother did not tell the teachers and I think she was always afraid to tell anyone about Ethan's anger in fear she would lose him; or I think she was so shut down that she may not have even seen it going on. After all, as soon as I could leave in the morning, I was out of that house and did not come home until my mother asked me to for bedtime. My mom was doing her best to cope.

Continue; The Semi-Colon

The semi-colon tattoo is on my left forearm. It is the "I" in the word "continue". The semi-colon is part of a movement called the semi-colon project which raises awareness for mental health illness. The semi-colon, in the English language represents a pause, not an ending to a sentence. In the mental health realm and the discussion of suicide, a semi-colon represents the pause in your story, but not the end. I have the semi-colon tattooed in the word continue to represent my battle with suicide. The "continue" reminds me to keep moving forward. And the birds that blossom out of the semi-colon represent freedom from the demons, when I was finally able to talk about my suicide experiences openly. I tried to commit suicide twice in my life.

I played sports in middle school including basketball and track and field. I remember my mother coming to maybe 4 games/ track meets. Yes, I understand she was a single mother who was a teacher, but it hurt never having family support there and seeing everyone else's parents making the effort. She would drop me off at most of my in town games, until I could drive. Most of the time, I would get home from a meet or game and she would be back in her hole on the computer or the couch, with the empty eyes. My friends' parents would always cheer me on, and it always gave me comfort to as least know someone cared. As 7th grade came to an end, and then 8th, and I entered high school, I continued to hide what was going on at home. I can't write about any good memories I have with my mother or Ethan. I don't remember many conversations with my mother other than discussing homework occasionally or dinner for the night. The end of middle school into high school was a huge transition for me as a teenage girl, but was also a turning point for my emotional stability.

I entered high school and decided I would do the same thing, bury myself in extra curricular activities and stay close to my friends. I would only go home once it was dusk and the sun was setting. This was because that would mean my mother would be home and Ethan was less likely to beat me up, scream at me or remind me of how worthless I was. Not to say it did not happen when she was home. There were plenty of times Ethan would scream at me in my face and hit me and my mother would be home, but I think she had no energy to really stand up to someone who, by this time, was bigger and stronger. My mother was broken—she was broken emotionally and I think deep down she felt like she had nothing left to fight for after losing Noah. She was so numb to pain, she couldn't see the pain Ethan and I were feeling. Ethan also wasn't just cruel to me, he was cruel to her. He would scream at her and threaten her. I think after years of that, she became scared of him too. There was no reason she would stand up to him if it meant losing another child, even if it meant I had to endure the threats, and the pain from Ethan. She was gone. Her soul was broken, and I needed to just survive until I could leave.

High School is already a tough place for a teenager, whether you are a girl or a boy. It's a time when everyone is comparing each other to one another. I stayed involved in high school with sports and band. Anything to keep me out of that house. I knew I did not dress the prettiest or have the best clothes. With my mom being so into her depression, she never taught me how to do my make up or about getting your eyebrows tweezed, things like that, so I always was made fun of for my clothes by other girls. I had a group of friends that stuck with me and most of them were the band students or jocks from the track team. My brother Ethan had made me believe I was ugly inside and out, so I already felt way below the scale against the other girls in high school with me. My best way to survive it was to stay with the things I was comfortable in, and that was band and sports. I did pretty well during freshmen year, I made a group of friends in band and joined the track team. I still hung out with Joey and our group of friends after school and I continued to focus on my academics. I wasn't bullied too much outside of the occasional comments from girls about how I dressed or the way I looked. Not having a close relationship with my mother, led me to having no idea what to do when I first got my period. A lot of girls were dating and to me, the boys I was friends with were my buddies and more like brothers. I also had no confidence when it came to boys. I was ugly and I constantly compared myself to the other girls in high school around me. So I did not really look into dating or really know how to "do" it. Even sex, that was a whole other mystery to me again, because I never had the talk with my mom about what sex was and being safe. All in all, I was a pretty uncomfortable person in high school, but I did my best to hide it.

Freshmen year flew by, and it was weird to see some of Noah's friends as upperclassmen. Some of them would come up to me and ask me how my brother was and I always said he was good. I never knew what to say and it always made me sad. That summer after freshmen year, I spent it most of it at band camp. Marching up and down the football field learning all of the steps and movements for the upcoming fall season where we would compete against other bands across the United States as well as perform at the home football games. I continued to build a tight friendship group within the band.

I always looked up to the drum majors who would lead the band, teach us how to march, and conduct the music. I wanted to be the drum major one day, I remember thinking to myself as a freshmen. So I started talking to the upperclassman in band and trying to learn what it took to become the drum major. I remember a girl named Sue was the drum major I first told my aspirations to. I admired Sue and she mentored me while she was at Lyman Hall by giving me tips on how to become a drum major. I then started to volunteer to do a lot of the extra clean up tasks at night and stick around after practices. After all—I did not want to go home. Eventually someone noticed it.

He was the band director and my freshmen year was his first year as such. He was young and cool to me. He drove the cool car and was always nice to all of us. He seemed fun and outgoing and I knew that if I wanted to be drum major, I had to impress him. He was the person who also had a big say in who became drum major. So I started to build a good friendship with him when I would ask for advice on how to improve myself as a musician and as a leader. At this time, no one had any idea still about the abuse back home and I always thought I would keep it that way.

I still am not sure exactly how it happened, but one day I remember walking into the band director's office and he asked me why I always stayed so late. I remember telling him about how I did not like going home because of my brother. I did not tell him the extent but I just remember he was one of the first people I confided in. This was the beginning of accepting that I needed to talk to someone about what was going on. As an adult looking back I realized that at this time was when I was beginning to comprehend a little bit of what had happened to me over the last 6 years. That it may not be right to be avoiding my home all the time. I realized I was hiding from my feelings. I knew that if I showed feelings at home around Ethan it usually ended in a screaming fight towards me or if I tried to talk to my mom to express my fears or sadness, she would not respond. So when he asked me a simple question, I replied with the truth, and realized that truth was not a normal answer.

Aside from making friends in band, I had made a friend in high school named Colby. He was the handsome upperclassman that played football that everyone loved. And I definitely thought he was cute, but I knew I had no chance of dating him. He lived close by to where I did and I would see him around with one of my friends, Tommy. Tommy hung out with Joey, he and I volunteered with Colby at a local haunt. "The Trail," as we called it, was a local haunted attraction in our town that was started by a couple who created a haunted house at their house and gave the donated proceeds to the American Red Cross. I remember being in middle school and it was the cool place to go when you got older around Halloween time. The Trail had grown too large for the couple's house and it moved from their house to a location across town. Tommy and Colby both told me to come down there and check it out. They both told me a lot of people volunteer there to building it in the off season and that everyone who was there were good people. Eventually, it intrigued me and I remember taping my CD player to the front of my Mongoose blue BMX bike and riding the 3 miles down to the Trail to check it out. When I arrived it was full of people painting different scenes that were all based off of different horror stories and movies like "SAW" or "IT." During October, the scenes recreated popular moments from the movies and came to life, staffed by actors and actresses who were volunteers. The volunteers would work on the set all off season and then scare during Halloween to raise money for the American Red Cross. So I started to ride my bike down there after school or on weekends to hang out with Tommy and Colby and to volunteer when I could during the fall season.

I was looking forward to the fall and the football games and bus trips. I was 15, about to turn 16 in January. I was going through the social changes of high school, as well as trying to avoid going home. I was processing what my older brother told me regularly about my appearance and worth. He always made sure to let me know I was ugly, and worth nothing. He reminded me I was the reason my brother left the family. He would make fun of my smile and the way I looked. Towards the end of the summer, I realized, I could not hide "it" anymore. By "it" I mean my sadness.

As the summer came to an end I started cutting my left arm. Many people who have never experienced mental illness will not know what it feels like to want to do that to yourself, to self-mutilate. It's because I could not feel pain, I could not cry after my brother would scream at me, or call me horrible things. I could not feel happiness because I was not sure what it was, I did not know what love was. I could not express sadness, and I wanted to feel something. I am not sure when I did it, but I remember I found an X-acto knife in my mother's desk drawer and I placed it on my skin. I made a cut. The first slice did not do much. But then I ran the blade back and forth a few more times, in a sawing motion. Finally I felt it. I felt pain. I saw blood. I felt like I was alive. I did not cry in pain, I just remember I would sit there and just feel. And that's all I wanted to do…was to feel. I started to do this regularly towards the end of that summer and I would hide the cuts with my shirts or with sweat bands. Not a single one of my friends knew. This was the beginning of my depression. Sure, you always hear about teenagers going through depression because of bullying and the social pressures, but I think I had those social pressures combined with not feeling any worth. My mother had not said 'I love you' to me in years or hugged me, or said "good job"; instead I had my brother reminding me over and over of the failure I was and how ugly I was. He would call me "maggot." I learned that if I showed emotion in those interactions with him, I was losing. So cutting and self-mutilation were my only ways to express myself as I never wanted to be perceived as weak.

Within a few weeks my depression spiraled. Looking back, I think I always had the depression developing, but it was coming to a head at this point. I felt like I was just waiting to explode. I did not know it then, but I was. I continued to go to band practice and school and act normal, but I remember I had to consciously put on a show and act my normal self, as to not stir up anything. And then I couldn't pretend anymore.

It was beginning to get cold, and I remember the river that was near my house. I could easily walk to it. I never looked up ways to commit suicide but I knew that drowning or hypothermia were not as vulgar looking. So I remember cutting my arm, and then walking to that river. I went and I sat by it and cried. I cried the first tears I had in years and I just said to myself in a low voice "you are worth nothing and no one loves you." I jumped into the river. Luckily for me, the river was not deep, but it was cold. I figured eventually I would freeze and float downstream. As I laid there in the river, I am not sure what stopped me, but I got up I pulled myself out. I think I was scared but I truly do not remember. Scared to die? Maybe. I walked in and I wrote my mom a note. A suicide note. I remember her coming home and finding me in her room as I was leaving it for her. She still had not seen the marks on my wrists, but I looked at her and cried out "I don't want to be here anymore" and I dropped to the floor. She called 911 and I was taken to the hospital.

I was admitted into the children's psychiatric unit at Yale New Haven Hospital. I was the second oldest child in the unit. I was not allowed near any sharp objects, had a set TV time, and set therapy sessions. I was allowed visitors as long as I followed the rules. I was 15 and horrified. I remember feeling so sad and missing the comforts of my home, but at the same time, I liked having someone to talk to. And when I say comforts of home, I really just meant my bed, and my belongings. I hated the sanitary environment of the hospital ward. The therapist met me when I first was taken in and I explained how I was feeling and that it was the first time I had tried to take my life. But I remember saying, "I just want to feel wanted and loved". I described how my mother was never around and was very depressed, how my brother Noah left. I explained how my mom's illness uprooted us all and how Ethan acted towards me. The therapists asked what I thought could help and I said I just want my mom to go to therapy with me and show me love, that is all. I want to have a family again. I told the therapist I missed having the holidays and eating at the table all together. I told her about the adoption and she explained that adoption in itself causes abandonment feelings let alone when a family faces trauma that causes separation from parents. The therapist would brief my mother every time she visited. I remember it was September because it was my mom's birthday on one of the visit days and I felt bad for having her in the hospital with me.

I remember the other kids that were there with me and the issues they were trying to work on being much more grave than mine in comparison. That probably sounds crazy given I had tried to take my life, but it seemed as though they had handled their own struggles differently, whereas I had put all of my effort into school and academics to stay afloat. I remember feeling sad for them to see them struggle with things much worse than what I thought I was battling. I watched as they lashed out in anger and fought with the doctors. The worst thing I experienced while I was there was crying at night until I was able to understand I was valued after numerous intense therapy sessions.

When my mom would visit, she was allowed to bring me a snack and she always brought me vanilla ice cream with chocolate chips. She also brought me my school work. Not only was I terrified to fall behind in school, but I was more terrified as to what kids were saying about me.

I was allowed to make phone calls while I was there and I called Colby and Brittany. They were the two that knew I was there and stood by me. They told me what kids were saying about me and how I was crazy and suicidal and a whack job. It hurt knowing that but I was in a psych ward.

I luckily was able to show I was not a threat to myself but I needed intense therapy WITH my mother. My mother agreed to it and I was able to return home after about two weeks of being in the program. I was excited and thought my mom would soon join me in my healing process. She came to one therapy session with me and never came again. I slipped back into my depression but I was careful to hide it and try and find ways to work through it based on what I had learned in my treatment program.

Going back to high school that fall was tough. Everyone knew I was hospitalized and why, and no one knew what happened in my household when I was younger or what was happening at that present time. I was judged and I lost a lot of friends that year. But it also made me stronger. I had to learn to survive alone at a young age and I was used to losing people by this time, so I just continued along. I kept attending counseling sessions at school and my teachers all knew about the incident so they would monitor and check in with me periodically. My pre-algebra teacher was by far, my favorite high school teacher because he was so kind and always could tell if I was having an off day emotionally. He would say something positive directly to me, to make sure I knew I was a good kid inside. And those little sentiments that he, and many of my teachers unknowingly said, are what got me through most of my days in high school.

My home life stayed the same, so I just continued my routine of staying late at school and participating in extra-curricular activities like track and band to keep me from going home before my mom would get there. I also kept volunteering at the Trail on the weekends. I put all of my energy into school and sports. This kept Ethan's interactions with me on the lower side during the week. But I felt myself slipping back into that depression in November. I knew I needed to talk to someone but I did not trust anyone. Until one day at the Trail.

Gracie Rising: The Scars Beneath

End of Silence

"Terminus Silentium" loosely translated in Latin means "end of silence". End of Silence is a slogan for a child abuse campaign that encourages people who were victims to talk about what happened to them. The tattoo covers the cutting scars on my forearm that became raised in the summer. I got this tattoo years after I first told my story to someone when I was 15. I got this tattoo when I was finally able to process everything as an adult and needed to force myself to share my story to help myself, and help others. It was one of my earliest tattoos, and it was when I decided I would use my ink to talk about my life, and paint my story without being afraid to talk about it anymore. At the time of this tattoo, I realized talking about my past to others when asked, was healing for me.

Who was that someone that got me to open up? His name was Will. One day I was painting a black fence at the Trail in November of my sophomore year and a nice, older guy who I had seen around the Trail many times before came over to me and struck up a conversation. I had my headphones on and I removed them to engage in conversation with him. Per usual I put on a happy face and pretended to be perfectly fine. I had interacted with him a few times with Colby and Tommy and I knew Will was close to them. He was always nice to all of the volunteers and always smiling, so I liked being around his cheery personality. We chatted for a few minutes about school and the Trail. At some point he stopped and looked at me and said "I see hurt in your eyes". That phrase to this day I will never forget. And just like that, I told him my story. Over a few days of hanging around him I opened up like I never had. Eventually I would go to the Trail to volunteer and talk to Will because I trusted him and he was a good listener. Eventually I met his wife, Charlotte who was a very sweet person and they both had huge hearts. Come to find out, they were the owners. I was with them both almost daily by the end of the fall and into the winter.

Once the Trail would close down for the winter, and was all boarded up until spring, all of the volunteers would go see the latest horror movies, attend haunt conventions, and take trips to other haunts all in preparation for the next Trail season. Will and his wife would throw an end of the season Trail party and all of the volunteers would come and he would give out awards to the volunteers. At that party I met Colby's older brother Ricky, and we became close friends. Ricky and Colby lived next to Will and Charlotte and soon I became a staple between the two houses. Ricky and I grew close that winter and he and Will taught me how to drive, in addition to the limited hours I drove with my mother. Eventually I was at Will and Charlotte's house so much that I looked at them as second parents. I loved being with them. They were always sure to tell me how much they cared about me and gave me the sense of belonging I needed at that time in my life. Will eventually noticed the cuts on my arm were coming back and he began to check my arm regularly when I would see him. When he saw they were coming back we would talk a lot and he would make sure I was going to see my therapist. He even came to a session. I was cutting again because I was still at home most of the time and I was still fighting with my brother and the conflicting feelings of not being loved. Although Will and Charlotte were good at expressing feelings to me, I was still struggling on how to accept love and how to express it. I was also scared. I did not want to get hurt. I did not know what I was feeling at times and I was confused with if I was supposed to love people who are not my parents, by society's rules. I told Will I thought of him as a dad to me and I wanted him to walk me down the aisle when I get married. They did not have kids of their own and eventually a lot of people at the Trail knew I looked at Will as my dad. The Trail people began to call me "BC"…short for "band camp" because whenever I wasn't at the Trail during the daytime. I was always at band camp. Will and Charlotte welcomed me into their family and I spent that Christmas with their families and friends. I felt badly not being home, but I felt happier being with Will and Charlotte. At some point I was over at their house so much that I was asked to ask my mother's permission to stay there from time to time. So I did. She did not blink or hesitate when I asked. She knew who they were and knew they were good people, but she did not care to think that I was pulling away from my home for any reason. So I stayed there on and off during my sophomore year of high school and into my junior year. They threw me a surprise sweet 16 and I had not had a birthday party since I was very young that I could remember. That was the best gift, when I arrived at the bowling alley to go bowling with Ricky, I opened a curtain and all of my closest friends surrounded me to celebrate my birthday. That summer Will and Charlotte took me to Disney in Florida and Clearwater beach where I felt my happiest. I loved them so dearly and I couldn't understand why they were so good to me. We continued to grow closer and Will continued to watch my arm. I know there were a few times I cut when I was back at my mom's and he was hurt that I did that, and I hated making him feel so upset. He explained to me he did not want me on medications to help my depression because he truly believed I could be happy without them. He believed I just needed to think the right way and surround myself with the right people. I have stuck to that philosophy back then, and still to this day, even when things got really tough with my depression. I was on medication for a short period of time during high school after my first suicide attempt, but the medication made me numb and zombie-like. I was and still am forever grateful for having Will and Charlotte in my life. I never thought I would lose them, but I did. Not to any tragedy, but to my own demons.

I became very dependent on Will and Charlotte as my source of love and the sense of belonging during those middle years of high school. By the fall of my junior year, I had not fully processed all that had happened to me before Will and Charlotte were in my life. There was another girl at the Trail who started volunteering who had recently lost her dad. I noticed she started to get close to Will and I began to feel threatened. Looking back now, I have been able to process and assess those feelings I was experiencing when I saw them getting close. I was getting jealous. I was so scared to lose the person I called dad, and the first two people to show me a happy life. And I flipped out. I remember it being late and cold at the Trail that night, and I did not know how to express my feelings of jealousy or that I felt like I was going to lose Will and Charlotte. I remember saying something so mean to Will in regard to him not loving me. I remember I couldn't say 'I love you' to Charlotte but I could say it to Will, because I felt like I was betraying my mother in some way. When in reality, I loved Will and Charlotte more than I did anyone in my own family. A few days later I apologized, but it was too late. I was asked to leave the house. They decided it was better for me to go back home and work things out with my mother. Our communication began to fade and we did not see each other as much. I was not invited out any more with their family and many of my calls, text messages and instant messages would go unanswered. I wrote many letters apologizing and explaining what I thought my rationale was at the time. I am not even sure if they ever read them. Much of those letters said I was sorry and I did not know how to handle my emotions at that time. But I knew I had made a huge error and lost the people who cared about me the most.

Will came to my senior powderpuff football game, most of my home track meets and high school graduation, but as soon as I graduated, it was if I was erased from Will and Charlotte's lives.

During this time, I had begun two jobs, one at the local YMCA and the other at the local movie theater. I would run into Will and Charlotte at the movies and we would make eye contact, and then their backs would turn. I tried to apologize in person and explain my side but I knew I had hurt them too deeply.

I do not regret our relationship or all of the lessons they taught me in life. As an adult, I have tried to make amends, but I still was denied. I eventually had to accept he will not walk me down the aisle. I used to dread that day, being walked down the aisle without him, but now, at 31 years old, I cannot let that ruin a day that will be one of the best moments of my life. It took me over 10 years to let go, without closure, but I am forever grateful for that chapter of my life. They taught me how to love unconditionally and to believe in myself.

Dating started to pique my interest towards the end of high school. I met an older guy who worked at the YMCA with me and we started dating. He was from Wallingford and going to school to be a teacher. He was my first real boyfriend. I did not know what to expect but I knew I was used to the way my brother Ethan treated me. When he, my former boyfriend, and I would argue, I thought it was normal. He hated how I would never want to be around my mother and often times he would say I was crazy for being so angry towards her. At times she would say cruel things as I was walking out the door and I would respond. My ex boyfriend would hear my response and just took it to imply I was cold-hearted and mean. He never cared to ask me why I was so angry, but eventually he just told me I was crazy. It wasn't a good relationship and my friends began to tell me he was emotionally abusive as it moved into college. Eventually I discovered he was talking to other women and once my trust was broken, that was the end of my relationship with that person. That became the theme of my adult life- trust.

I did not let the loss of Will and Charlotte deter me, I kept pushing through high school without letting on to anyone that inside I was hurting a lot. I went back to the status quo of working hard in academics and extra-curricular activities and keeping my feelings and my home life very quiet. I was terrified to open up again and then lose the person or people I opened up to.

I joined the track team freshmen year of high school and continued throughout my senior year. I was the captain my senior year. I excelled in track during high school. The 100m hurdles were my main event. I was a good sprinter and won numerous meets. I even tied my high school record. It gave me great pride knowing I was good at track.

I was the President of the Key Club in high school. Key Club was all about volunteering and helping the community, which I loved doing. I had been a member for two years before becoming President. It kept me busy on the weekends and days after school.

I became one of three drum majors senior year, a goal I had since freshmen year. I remember practicing every weekend before the tryout and discussing how to prepare with all of the senior leaders in band the year leading up to the big try-out.

For the first time in a very long time, when I was named one of the drum majors, I felt like I accomplished something. I felt like I was good at something, and it was because I did it without people telling me what to do. I made the decisions to ask for advice and to practice. Looking back, I think this was one of the first times I saw that I could control certain things in my life, outside of my family. I could be happy in other aspects of my life.

During my senior year of band, I finally realized what gave me the most joy — helping others. There was a sophomore who was wearing wristbands all the time, and always staying at band late. One day I went over and asked her if she was ok and I saw her wrists uncovered. I saw her scars. I showed her mine, and I told her I understood what she was going through. We became friends and built a trust over our secret. I introduced her to some of my friends and always kept a pulse on how she was doing. I always was sure to say hi to her and wish her happy holidays, etc. to make sure she knew someone cared about her.

After some of our conversations, I began to worry about her safety. I realized I was doing her no favor keeping my concerns to myself. I was worried she would hate me for breaking her trust. I had to let the band director know about what was going on. She eventually went and got help from a professional and came back flourishing. I went on to graduate, but I kept in contact with her. She ended up making a lot of friends in band and using it as an outlet. Her confidence grew and she felt like she belonged. I was happy for her. And for me, I realized I could help people by sharing my story. At least the story of my battle with depression and suicide at this point. At this point in my life, that was the only battle I really faced. I was not totally ready to walk around talking about my suicide at that moment in my life, but I kept it in the back of my mind. But I had no idea that all of the other things I experienced would become experiences that could help others as well.

I got accepted to a university in Connecticut. From the time my mother lost Noah to the state system and I watched her depression worsen, I had decided my lifelong dream was to be an FBI Agent. I knew that the only thing that could possibly bring my mother out of her depression was being reunited with my brother Noah. I wanted to find my brother and the FBI was the best at finding people. There was a billboard on interstate 95, picturing a forensic scientist who worked at the University that captured my attention. After visiting campus, I liked the small class size, which allowed for more focus on students from the teachers, unlike a lot of the larger state schools. I wished it was further from my hometown but I knew I could live on campus and not home anymore. Being private though, I knew I was in trouble.

My mom could barely offer any financial assistance so I knew I would have to foot the bills in student loans the majority of time as well as private scholarships. I also knew I would have to maintain a job during college to help pay my bills. I was determined to achieve my dream. In the fall of 2006, I entered the University as a freshmen in the Criminal Justice program. I intended to take classes in the summer at the local community college to save money and to live on campus to finally be away from my brother Ethan. I moved in that August.

College gave me a chance for a fresh start with people who did not know who I was or my past. After my sophomore year in high school was full of judgement, a new start was just what I needed. The first semester I lived in a small dorm, which had suite-style living. The dorm was away from the main freshmen dorms that were in the "quad". That first semester I did not venture far from my routine of classes and being in my dorm room. I did not know where the quad was until late in the semester and realized that is where all of the freshmen hung out. That first semester was an adjustment to living away from home and getting used to college level classes and independence. I was also on the track team, so I was adjusting to multiple workout sessions, early wake ups and classwork. I handled it well, but stayed pretty quiet that first semester. Track kept me motivated and active. After my first year, I ended up dropping off the track team to keep up with my academics. I knew that I was not going to be a professional athlete and I needed to focus on paying bills and doing well academically. It was a very hard decision, but in the end, it was the best decision for me.

The second semester of my first year, I met a few girls in my suite who were part of a sorority. I never saw myself as the sorority girl, at least not the ones I would see on TV. I was still working back in Wallingford at the YMCA and the movie theater so I was not sure I would be able to work between classes, keep up with my school work, and be in a sorority. I was always friends with guys, because we all had similar interests, mainly sports, so I was not used to hanging around a lot of girls. I met a few of the girls and we became friends but I still was not totally sold on the idea of being in a sorority. I felt awkward with the way I looked, and I was very self-conscious. I always thought you had to be pretty or "hot" to be in a sorority and at that time in my life, I viewed myself as being far from either of those.

I made one of my first friends during my first year at the University. His name was Erick. We were in the same class and after we had gotten a test back, he asked me if I would be interested in studying with him. I soon realized he too was very good academically and we had similar goals. We both had to pay for school by working and both of us needed to attend community college to save money. We both ended up taking classes together at the community college the summer after freshmen year. We both started to hang out all the time and joined the Criminal Justice Club. We both were selected to go to Washington DC as freshmen because we were good students and our advisors selected us based on our contributions to the club. That apparently was an accomplishment in the eyes of the advisors. "CJ Club" was made up of primarily criminal justice majors. The club participated in community service events and would set up speaker series on campus, where law enforcement professionals from state, local and federal agencies would come and speak on current affairs topics in the law enforcement field. It was a good club to be part of for professional networking. I saw it as a positive stepping stone towards the FBI.

I stopped working at the YMCA and movie theater during my second year of college because I was not making enough income to justify the commute back and forth to Wallingford. I began working at Abercrombie and Fitch and became a building supervisor at the new Recreation Center on campus. In order to support myself financially I worked those jobs while in school. Both jobs were flexible with my class schedule and I was able to earn enough income to pay some of my tuition and my bills.

By this time I was becoming much more involved on campus between the CJ Club, and hanging out with the sorority sisters to figure out if it was something I really wanted to join. Working at the Recreation Center also expanded my friend group. A lot of people knew I was one of the supervisors at the Recreation Center and a member of the special events committee on campus that helped with our spring weekend. During spring weekend, I was one of the students who would assist in escorting the musical artists around. People knew that, so if people wanted to know where they would be, I would get asked.

I started building a large group of friends from all different backgrounds on campus. I played in the basketball league where I was one of the few females who could hold their own against the boys. By the end of my second year I was non-stop busy with social events, club meetings, working off campus, and my academics. I ended up becoming a member of the Phi Sigma Sigma sorority in spring 2008 because a lot of the sisters were criminal justice majors and we had similar motivations. I was coming out of my shell. Phi Sigma Sigma had a heavy community service element and did not seem to be the stereotypical sorority from television. Joining the sorority introduced me to a whole other group of people, some of which would become my roommates my second year at school.

The one thing Abercrombie did bring me was a new sense of fashion. For the first time in my life, I did not buy baggy clothes to hide my insecurities of my body. It was recommended we wear the company's clothes and dress to their brand while at work. So I started wearing their clothes, which forced me to care a little more about the way I looked. I felt uncomfortable at first, but with the discount I got on the clothes, I slowly became comfortable in the clothing since it was paying the bills.

I ended up leaving my job at Abercrombie and Fitch after about six months and working at a local bar in New Haven because I did not like working retail anymore. I liked interacting with my friends at the bar and meeting people. I loved staying busy. The bar was still a better move as I was able to work three nights a week and I made more money.

I met my college boyfriend shortly after leaving my job at Abercrombie and Fitch. Ironically, he commented on my Abercrombie style when he first talked to me in a class we had together. He was from Connecticut and he was the first person I told a lot of my insecurities to, not all of them, but I did tell him about my past depression. He seemed to understand it and was always very understanding. He would take the time to talk to me when I was upset about family stuff back home and never judged me. If I had to go home for a weekend, and my brother acted out towards me, he was always there for me when I would come back to let me talk it out. He was thoughtful and never yelled at me or argued with me like my previous ex, but he too ended up cheating on me numerous times. By the beginning of my last year in my undergraduate program, he and I had split. I was pretty angry with him because I did care a lot about him and he broke my trust. I told him things I did not tell anyone and once that trust was broken, I was not sure I could ever trust him again. It hurt because I knew he truly understood and accepted what I had gone through before college, especially my depression and feelings of loneliness. He knew I hated to be alone. But I could not handle my trust being broken. I closed my feelings back up into a deep bubble.

I was pretty sad after the break up, but that is when I leaned on my sorority sisters. They helped me through it and I was back on my feet. I even was persuaded to enter the Phi Sig Swimsuit contest on campus. I ended up winning which shocked me! I was convinced I won because I could throw a football as a talent. My confidence about my body was growing slowly. Towards the end of my second year at college, I realized I was on track to graduate early.

Erick and I had been attending summer and winter classes at community college and I also studied abroad twice. I was minoring in Arabic Language and Cultural Studies to hopefully make me a more competitive applicant for the FBI. At that time, Arabic was a good language skill to pick up post 9/11, so I wanted to make sure I did all I could to set myself up to get into the FBI after graduation. Between the two times I studied abroad, I traveled to Oman, Dubai, Egypt, and Jordan, where I was fully immersed into the language and culture the entire time I was there. It was a great experience to travel as well as learn cultures of other areas of the world. Between community college and the study abroad, I ended up fast tracking my timeline to graduate with my bachelor's degree in three years, versus four. Erick did the same.

I continued to look forward and was soon elected to be the President of the Criminal Justice club during my last year of undergraduate school. Erick was elected to be the Vice President, standing alongside me. I remember thinking to myself "this last year was going to be great." I kept my eyes set on the FBI. By this time I had completed an internship in the Major Crimes Division of a local police department, which gave me exposure to how local law enforcement worked violent crimes in the Connecticut area.

I left my job at the bar and began working another job on campus at the Institute for the Study of Violent Groups or ISVG. This was a DOD contracted research program the late Dean brought to the University. There I would review open source articles and enter data into a DOD database for statistical purposes. I knew this would be helpful for applying to the FBI as articles I was reviewing were of interest to the FBI. I was gaining skills in data entry. This was a skill I knew that was needed to be an Intelligence Analyst for the FBI. Although I did not dream of being an Intelligence Analyst, I knew it would be a good stepping stone to the FBI Agent career path. While I was at ISVG, and promoted to a data supervisory role, I started my application to the FBI internship program since it was my last year of undergraduate studies, given my expected early graduation.

About 2 months after I applied for an internship with the FBI, I received an email saying I was selected for the next phase of processing. This consisted of a phone interview. I remember sitting and waiting for the phone to ring, unsure of what was going to come. It rang and my heart was pounding! The questions they asked me were mostly what I had expected for the internship but it felt like the entire world was on my shoulders with every answer. After the phone call, I felt pretty good about how it went.

A month later I was contacted stating I had passed the interview and would begin the background process. I then had to fill out the SF-86. The SF-86 was about 100 pages of information about all of my life. Then it was time to wait until the next update. I was nearing the end of my undergraduate program and I asked around about how long the process would take. One of my advisors stated it would take up to a year, if not more. That was when I started to toy with the idea of getting a Master's Degree. I figured having a Master's degree would possibly lead to better pay and would make myself more competitive for the FBI.

At this point I was finally feeling like my life was going somewhere and I was gaining a new confidence in myself both personally and academically. I was excelling in academics and had built a strong network of friends at the University. I was leading clubs on campus and was well known in the Recreation Center and at ISVG. People would come to me for help and advice and I loved helping out. I was so focused on school and succeeding, so that I could have my dream career that I rarely deterred from my game plan. I was not one to go out and party or attend the biggest events on campus, mainly because I was usually working and I did not want to get caught up in anything that could jeopardize my career or background investigation for the FBI. But one night, I decided I deserved to let loose. I was 21 years old and I wanted to go to one of the parties on campus. There were a few of my friends going so we all decided to go together. It was the fall before I was going to graduate with my bachelor's degree. I did not drink alcohol even though I was of age because I learned early on that alcohol was a depressant. I knew that I had underlying depression and that drinking would only make it worse, even when I worked at the bar in New Haven, I chose not to drink. I still decided to go out to the party and have some fun.

I don't remember the day, maybe a Friday or Saturday, or even the exact details looking back 10 years, but I do remember I was at the residence hall where the guy lived after the party. He was a guy I recognized from around campus. He was a good-looking guy and on one of the athletic teams at the University. I really had only ever slept with people I had dated up to this point so I did not expect anything when we ended up at the same party together earlier in the night. I had been at the party maybe 2 hours. I ate some snacks and drank some water. My friends were off talking to their friends when the guy from the sports team approached me. We started talking and it led to harmless flirting. We exchanged phone numbers and continued the flirting. I was not expecting him to be interested in me at all. I ended up leaving the party and heading back to my dorm.

A bit of time passed and I eventually went back to his dorm to visit some other friends. I texted him when I was headed back over, and we continued our flirtatious conversation. I remember him inviting me up to his apartment once I got to the dorm. I was pretty nervous about it, but I gave a nod to my friends I was visiting and walked up to the guys dorm room/ apartment. We walked into his room and he made a move to kiss me. I kissed him back but I did not think it would go much further. He kept kissing me, and eventually went up my shirt. He fumbled with my belt, being that he was intoxicated, and I helped him undo it. I got nervous at first because I was not sure I wanted to have sex with someone I was not dating, but at that point I was fine with seeing where it went. He took off my pants and underwear on the bed. He straddled me and then jumped off the bed to take off his shirt, shorts and boxers. He grabbed a condom. He slipped on the condom and we began to have intercourse.

That first few minutes were fine, and I agreed to what was happening, but as it went on, I found it to be forceful and aggressive. I was in pain. I attempted to tell him how my head was being slammed against the wall as he was thrusting into me, but he did not respond. As he was on top of me, he lifted my legs onto his shoulders and continued to slam his body inside of mine, I told him to stop. I felt my muscles strain in my legs. My right hip began to feel pain and whenever I told him, he just switched positions. At the current day, I cannot recall how long it lasted, but I continuously vocalized the pain I was in. I asked him to stop. I faked orgasms and moans to help him get off, just so he would "finish" and I could go. I never felt like I could get up and just walk away, because he was stronger than me. I was no longer "wet" so every time he moved inside and out, it burned. When his door opened in the middle of it, I wanted to call for help to the person who peeked in, but I was afraid of how I would be viewed by other students. He continued switching positions, and eventually tried to anally penetrate me and then forced me to do oral on him. I remember looking up at him and crying during oral. He tried to vaginally penetrate me without a condom at one point and I told him no. Eventually it was over. As soon as he ejaculated, I got up and looked for my clothes. I couldn't find my pants and he could not either. He gave me a pair of shorts and I asked him to walk me to the door to avoid feeling everyone looking at me. I had no idea if they had heard me telling him to stop over and over again, or me saying he was hurting me.

I ran back to my dorm, and I called my friend. I asked him to come stay with me because I did not feel safe and I needed to tell him something. The next call was to my ex-boyfriend. I wanted to tell him exactly what happened because I knew he would not judge me or say anything to anyone. I asked him to go back and get the rest of my clothes and he did.

One of my friends in the fraternity, which was like the fraternity brothers to my sorority, heard I was upset about something and reached out to me. He came and talked to me and eventually told me he wanted me to report it to the campus police. I told him no over and over again. I told him cops never believe the victim, and that he's a popular guy on campus so I won't win. I told him I was scared. He said he would go with me and be there with me through it and that if I did not report it, he would, so we walked. I remember walking into campus police and being greeted with smiles by the people that knew me. The officers all knew me from campus because of my role as President of the CJ club. They did not think I was there to report it. I asked to speak to a female officer. I explained what happened to her and she explained that she needed to call the local police department for a sexual assault as it's not campus police's responsibility. I later found out, this avoids campus' reporting a sexual assault statistic on their campus.

Later that night, a male detective came in to interview me. I told him my background and who I was, and that I was applying to the FBI and had made it to the background stage. He seemed genuinely interested in learning what happened to me. After the interview, I cried and he told me I had to go to the hospital for a rape kit. So I went.

I was in the middle of the rape kit when the detective walked in and told the nurses to stop. By this point there was a campus victim advocate with me who was supposed to help me. She did not do that at all. The detective seemed angry and outraged. He said "I am going to tell the FBI what lies you have been telling me." He continued to hammer me with questions. He implied to me that I asked for it and never declined any of the actions this guy on campus took. I asked him if he had talked to any of my friends apart from just the friends of the male and he said he did not need to. He used terminology like "sweetie" and made me feel like I was at fault. I felt so empty inside.

I returned to campus and the following day I was called into the Dean of Students office. She had known me on campus and was familiar with me. She said she was aware of the situation. I thought she would be the understanding one and the one that was going to help me. She did not. She made rules and set boundaries for me. My work schedule had to be altered around the times that the male would use the gym to avoid running into him. I was not allowed near his dorm.

All of the resident hall assistants were notified and it was the equivalent of putting out a flyer with my face to all of my peers with the world to know what "I" had done. It spread quickly around campus. I reached out to my boss at the Recreation Center and told him something had happened and I needed to change my schedule. He was understanding and did not judge me for a second, and I am forever grateful for that. I did not want to leave my room. I did not want to see that guy on campus, or hear whispers about me. I did not want the eyes looking at me. I couldn't remember who was at the party, and I knew some guys had walked into his room during it but I did not know who they were. I felt empty. I stopped eating and I was losing motivation for anything including school. I called Erick and I told him what happened. I did not know how to tell the CJ club advisor that his President was taking a leave of absence. Erick ran the club for a few weeks and would bring me class assignments for the classes I was able to miss. Most of the teachers knew about what had happened but one professor was not so understanding. I asked to speak to him after class and he made me say out loud why I had missed a class the previous week. I did not say exactly what had happened out loud but I mentioned it was something very personal. I remember feeling the eyes of my classmates and feeling vulnerable in that moment. For three weeks I did not leave my room unless absolutely necessary. I thought about taking my life a few times. I felt worthless. I felt alone. But luckily, with the constant movement of people in and out of my dorm room and the fear of leaving my dorm, I was able to talk myself out of harming myself.

The semester ended and I had one semester left of undergraduate studies. I had taken a criminology class with a female instructor, who I admired a lot for her passion in helping victims. I walked into her office within days of the assault and told her what happened. She began to advocate for me both on campus, and off at the local police department. She got the CT Office of Victim Advocate involved. She fought for me in a meeting with the Chief of Detectives after the charges were dropped in my case. She was in the meeting with me when that Chief used inappropriate language with me and said that I should have just gotten up. She asked him if he knew what it felt like to be raped and he said no. She made it a point to make him see that there was no way he could tell me how I should have handled a situation he had never been in. Additionally, she got me a meeting with the prosecutor of the state of CT that was involved in my case. She continued to fight for me and eventually I was emotionally drained. I was let down by a system that did not work.

Years later, she described the "vacant" look I had on my face for months following the assault. She had always known me to be a voice on campus, a leader with a vibrant personality, and after the assault for months, she described me appearing as though I was about to "crack." I can only recall feeling like a zombie during this time, and blocking out much of the details of the assault in the coming years, but to hear her tell me years later that she had to choose her words carefully allowed me to understand the gravity this event had on me on my life. She had feared I was going to drop out of school, but now admired my strength following the assault. The only positive impact that I was able to make was the local department had to undergo a new sexual assault training, specifically related to how they speak to victims. I was terrified that detective called the FBI and that the one thing in my life that I had control of, was going to be taken away from me. With the support of Erick, my female advocate, and my ex, I was able to pick myself up and finish my undergraduate year strong. I even started dating another guy I had known for years. He had known me and asked me on a date a few months after this life- changing event happened to me. I was pretty disgusted with the idea of dating or touching a man, but agreed to a date since I had known him for so long. We began dating and when things moved into the serious route towards the end of my last semester, I remember breaking down crying. I had gotten a call from my female advocate regarding more information on the case, and the guy I was dating was also wondering why I would not be intimate. Well, I knew what I had to do. I had to tell this guy, who was putting his all into making me happy, that it wasn't him, it was me, as cliché as it sounds. To my surprise, he was the most understanding person I could have asked for to date after something like that. He said he would not force or do anything without my permission. He waited for a very long time for that wall to come down. To this day, I still have flashbacks and even when I see that guy around CT (because yes I have seen him), I go back into that hole I was in for a split second, but then I remember all the people that helped me and knew I did not ask for anything, and I pull myself out. I have nightmares at times, and intimacy issues when dating. I have some damage in my leg from it so it's always a conversation I have to have with the person I am with. And it's never easy. And I hate it, but over the last 10 years, I have learned to just talk about my story and help others. I have learned to take the bad times and use it as fuel to push on and be a better person. It gave me inner strength I did not know I had.

The late Dean awarded me a scholarship to continue my work with ISVG and obtain my Master's Degree at in National Security and Public Safety.

I began dating someone in January 2009 whom I had known for a few years. He had asked me out a few times and finally I gave in. He had stood by me during my flashbacks of the sexual assault in college and understood emotionally what I was going through. He was my best friend. His family had welcomed me as their own and I had grown close to his father. He was born and raised in Connecticut. He grew up in a family that was full of diversity so I never felt out of place or judged for having a split family. He never questioned my background or "scars" and just let me talk about things as I went. He allowed me to open up slowly as he did the same to me.

In the spring of 2009, I walked into a pet store with my boyfriend, and played with a cute little scruffy looking puppy. The puppy was a cairn terrier, and she was 6 months old. She was shy and timid in the playpen and was not like the other puppies. She was on sale. Although I had adopted animals when I was younger, and rarely thought about buying one, my adopted pets always ended up having a medical condition and we eventually had to put two of them down. I had always wanted to raise a puppy. I was afraid if this puppy was not purchased soon, she would be put down. I also think something about the idea of having a puppy need me and depend on me drew me to her. She reminded me of me, in some way, alone and timid. I went back that evening and purchased her without hesitation. I named her Justice. After a few weeks, she came out of her shell and her personality was electric. She went everywhere I went and was friendly to everyone. She protected me with her high-pitched bark and always was glued to my side. I kept her hidden from my mother for a while when she was a baby because I was unsure how she would react with a puppy in the home. Justice did not bark initially so it was easy to keep her a secret until she began to bark. Luckily, my mother had no issue with her as long as I was responsible for her. My mother did help from time to time with her if I was in class, but mostly she was my primary responsibility. I loved coming home and seeing how happy Justice was to see me. It made home a positive place for me, and I felt that I had a purpose at home. It was nice to have her love in return.

I graduated from my Bachelor's program in May of 2009. I began the Master's program that fall. At this time at the University, the Master's program was only a year long program, as it only consisted of three trimesters and an internship. I was able to get an internship at another local police department where I shadowed different officers and got experience working in the Evidence Control section of the department. My childhood friend's father was in a leadership position at that department and mentored me during my internship. All in all, school was going well and I was doing my best to stay busy while I waited for the FBI process to move forward.

I was lying in bed one morning with my boyfriend and I was scrolling through Facebook. I came across a post regarding a teenager who passed away in my hometown. I read on. Soon I realized, the teenager who passed away, was the little brother of my high school classmate. I was shocked. This family was well known in my town for their athletic talent and kind hearts. I could not imagine what they were going through. I decided to go to the funeral to show support for my classmate and his family. The line was out the door, full of current and former students. The teenager was set to graduate Lyman Hall in the summer. I saw my classmate and his family standing there. And my heart sunk. I hugged them each and offered my condolences. I also noticed some of my high school classmates there as well showing support, reminding me of how small our community was. I walked out and drove home.

I sat down with my boyfriend and I said to him, "I need to do something. I want to do something." I know what I experienced with Noah was not the same as it was for them at that moment, but I felt I needed to help. My brother left, and my family, at least for a short time knew where he was. They had lost their son to a tragedy. Regardless, I remember watching my mom mourn my brother, as she has done for years with not knowing where he is. I felt the loss of my middle brother, and saw how our family fell apart. I wanted to reach out to my classmate's family and say, "stay strong. Don't fall apart. You have two other great kids who need you." To show support, I decided I wanted to hold a basketball tournament in the town to raise money for a scholarship in his honor. But I wanted to make sure the family was OK with it. I don't remember how I did it, but I eventually met with my friend's father. I explained to him what I wanted to do and asked for his blessing. He gave it. I wanted the tournament to happen in June as it was around the time of his son's birthday and knew it would be a good time to host the tournament, before everyone went off for college and summer vacations.

In four weeks, I designed the tee shirts, secured multiple venues, and sold out the registration for the 3 on 3 basketball tournament. I worked with the family to make sure the event had input from them and paid tribute to their son. The town supported the tournament by donating their permits for the basketball courts. Referees volunteered their time since many of them knew the family. Restaurants, including Stella's, donated food for the tournament. My other high school classmate's family donated the banner, which was hung outside of the YMCA the day of the tournament. Flyers were posted all over social media and the town. The tournament exploded and was much larger than I had ever expected.

I had tons of the teenager's friends and their parents offering their help. The support was amazing. The tournament was a success and the money went into a scholarship fund in the teenager's honor. A few months later I explained to my friend's father how the loss of my brother effected my family and that I just wanted their family to know they had people there to support them. That summer I got the tattoo "BMAC", the teenager's nickname, under my brother's name on my neck. To honor his life.

In May 2010, I called the FBI to follow up on the status of my internship application. It appeared as though my SF-86 had fallen through the cracks. With the internship set to begin in June, they rushed my background and before I knew it, I was in the polygraph chair.

During the polygraph, I had to make sure they knew everything, including that I was estranged from my brother. That was a rough thing for me to do. I had to explain I had a brother who I did not talk to who I loved and was estranged from. And then I had to explain my adoption, my relationship with my mother, and Ethan. I had to explain it all to make sure I would have no doubts in answering any of the polygrapher's questions. It was hard to tell all this to a complete stranger, but I had to trust him without even knowing him. I did not want anything to stop me from achieving my dream.

After passing the polygraph stage, instead of the internship, I was offered a job as an Intelligence Analyst in Washington, DC. The date to report was unknown as I was still pending the conclusion of my background check, but it was anticipated it would be by the end of that year.

I spoke to my professors in the Master's program and explained I may have to leave for the FBI at the tail end of my last trimester. Within a matter of weeks of that discussion, a letter arrived from the FBI in Washington DC asking me to report in two weeks to Headquarters. I accepted the job. My professors and I worked out a way for me to do some extra work to make up for missing class time and I was able to complete my Master's degree remotely. I am so glad I was able to have the support from the faculty in the first steps to achieving my dream.

The FBI

On my left ribcage, inside the state of California, above the Hartford Whaler's logo, is a tattoo representing my dream of working for the FBI. The blueline flag draped down my left arm sleeve tattoo, in support of law enforcement.

I moved to DC in October 2010 and began my journey in the FBI. I was an Intelligence Analyst assigned to the Criminal Division in the FBI's headquarters office. I was making a starting government salary and living in Washington, DC. Financially, it was a tough move. My student loans from the University averaged about $1,000 a month. My rent was $1,500 a month. I was fortunate enough to have one of my professor's relatives rent me a place month to month on short notice just so I could report for work.

I lived on the college diet, the ramen noodle diet. Again, I decided to look at this new step in my life as a restart. I was far from my home and had control over every aspect of my life. I was able to choose whom I was around and how often I would go home. Given I was financially strained, I limited my travel back home to only when I wanted to see my boyfriend.

On my first day of work, I woke up with food poisoning and had to stop and puke in a trashcan at every metro stop. I remember sitting in the courtyard of the FBI building in my new black suit, white button up shirt, and new shoes. I sat alone, clinching my ginger ale and saltine crackers, hoping no one would talk to me. I had arrived early and after going through security, I was soon surrounded by many other young people excited for their first day of work.

A young girl, with gorgeous black hair came and sat next to me. She was stunning and smiley. She immediately spoke to me and said "cute shoes". I smiled and continued to keep to myself. I thought to myself "oh boy, this girl wants to be friends." Not that I was opposed to meeting new people, I was just very self conscious next to a girl as gorgeous as her. Her make up was on point and she dressed professionally and stylish. We made small talk about the process and before we knew it, all of us were being called one by one.

When my name was read, I smirked and giggled. When I stood up, the woman looked shocked that I was a petite Indian girl with such an American name. I was used to that reaction in general.

We all arrived in the same room filling out intake and insurance paperwork. That girl I had met down in the courtyard was next to me. Eventually I had to ask to leave as I continued to throw up. The human resources person understood my illness and asked me if I had anyone that could help me get home. I explained I knew no one. But was excused for the rest of the day. I had gone home sick on day one. I was pretty embarrassed.

The next day I reported to my unit. It was like a maze trying to learn my way around, but I was excited. The first week was full of meeting people, and briefings. I saw that girl I had met day one from time to time, but I could not remember her name. So I avoided eye contact a lot of the time to avoid embarrassing myself. I met Jeff and Calvin in my unit. And we became friends. The three of us were all around the same age. Calvin was a Yale graduate and was from California. He was dating a girl in Connecticut at the time so eventually we began to split the cost of gas and carpool together up there on weekends. Jeff was a graduate of the University of Illinois at Urbana Champaign. He had been there longer than Calvin and I and was very smart. He showed Calvin and I the in's and out's of our job. He had already been through his training at Quantico and Calvin and I were still awaiting our training date. There was an agent in my unit, a blonde female. She had an Alabama accent and her name was Kim. She asked me to do my first assignment on ATM Skimming. A project I thought was so random at the time, but years later has become quiet prevalent in financial crime today. I mentioned to her that I wanted to be an Agent down the line and throughout my time in the unit she answered a lot of my questions about being a Special Agent and being a woman in law enforcement. She became one of my first mentors in the FBI.

November 2010. I will never forget this month and year. I was finally feeling comfortable in DC. I was missing my boyfriend a lot but we were making it work. I was sitting at my desk and my phone went off. It was an unknown number from Waterbury, CT. I remember staring at it, and something in my body wanted to answer it, but I did not. A text follow up reading "answer my call, trust me." It rang again. I got chills down my spine. I answered the phone. "Hello?" I said. "Who is this?" The caller replied with "It's Noah." I froze. I did not know what to say back nor did I need to ask 'Noah who' as a follow up. I had done open source checks regularly for years to see if I could track down where my brother was. All I was able to find out from these checks is that he was in Connecticut and had ties to Waterbury, Stamford, Milford and Bridgeport. He hung up abruptly. I texted him back immediately and he said he could not talk.

I was in shock, to say the least. I had just started working for the FBI, and I still wanted to be an FBI Agent, and my brother calls. "What are the odds?" I thought to myself. I asked him where he was and he told me he was in Connecticut. I asked him how he had gotten my phone number and he recalled it being published in a newspaper along with my email. During the basketball tournament for Brian, the flyers with my contact information were printed around local newspapers throughout Connecticut.

I continued having conversations with Noah on my long drives back to Connecticut from DC, Noah asked me not to tell my mother that he had contacted me. I got engaged on Thanksgiving of 2010 to the man I was dating and told Noah that I wanted Noah to meet my fiancé. Even after all the years apart, I still felt closer and more trusting of Noah then I did to Ethan. I wanted Noah's approval of the man I was going to marry.

The only person I told about the reunion with my brother was my fiancé. I explained to him how I was overjoyed but also scared and nervous. I did not know how to handle this situation and I hated to keep it from my mother. I knew if my mother knew Noah was alive, it would help her. But I also knew that if Ethan found out I was talking to Noah, he would react the opposite way. I was more scared of that reaction.

Eventually, on one of the drives back to Connecticut, I figured out where Noah was. He was at a physical rehab facility recovering from an injury to his leg. I walked into the building, signed in as his sister and walked into his room. Describing how I felt and what I expected is impossible to do accurately. In my head, he was supposed to look the same as he did over 11 years ago. I expected him to be the same person I remembered. I walked in the room, I saw my brother's eyes, but his voice had deepened. He was a bigger man, with tattoos on his arms. He wore baggy clothes and a flat brimmed, fitted hat. We looked at each other. I wanted to cry, I wanted to smile, and I wanted to hug him. But I just stood there. And I let him speak. He took out a small box and inside of it was a stuffed animal dog that my mother had given him. He talked about how he had lived near my University and knew I ran track in high school and in College. I took all that he said in. I did not stay long, but I told him I was in town to see my fiancé. We agreed to meet up again and continue talking.

I walked out and got in my car. I called my fiancé. I told him I was coming over. At this time in my life, I still was not a crier. I grew accustomed to not showing emotion related to my family or around people in general. And I wanted to cry in my fiancés' arm when I got there, but I could not.

I remember one phone call with Noah on the many long drives back to DC. Noah told me how his life was at the state foster home. He told me about how he went back to Barbara and realized she was not a great person. He told me about how he had driven by the house on Backes Court a bunch of times but never could walk in. He told me about living on the street and getting caught up with the wrong people. He told me how his life was so hard because of what happened to him. He told me that I was lucky for having such an easy life. That was the only time I can say I got upset with him. For the first time, I expressed anger towards him. I explained to him that my life was not what he thinks. He painted my life as if I had it all. And yes, I had a roof over my head, and I wasn't starved to death, but I explained to him how when he left, the family turned upside down. I explained to him how mom's depression spiraled, and Ethan's anger took over. I explained how alone I felt. I am not sure he ever truly understood it, and I was not trying to blame him, but I wanted him to know. I remember feeling the pain on that phone call, pain I don't think I ever realized until that day. Lots of times after these calls, I would get back to my apartment and I would cry with Justice next to me. She was good and could always read when I was upset. She would just cuddle up next to me. She was what I needed during those times.

As time went on, I continued to work in DC and travel back to Connecticut to plan for the wedding and see Noah. It was July 2011, and the wedding was planned for 2012. I decided to come home for the 4th of July. When I was a kid, my mother used to take us to the Sheehan side of town around 4pm and stake out a good spot on top of the hill behind the school for the town fireworks. It was the best view in town for the fireworks but we had to get there early as it would get pretty crowded. My brothers and I, when we were young, we would play with sparklers and kick the soccer ball around in the field. We would also get to see our friends and then as soon as the finale would start mom would pack us up into the car to beat the traffic out of the school parking lot. I had not been back to Sheehan since I was about 11 years old, and decided that this year I wanted to go. My mom had been going for years alone and I was starting to feel bad with her being alone on holidays. I called Noah and asked him if he wanted to go with my fiancé and I. He declined.

My fiancé, my mother and I all went and it was a nice afternoon. My mom and I really did not talk much around this time in my life. She was very quiet, and just kept to herself. We were cordial most of the time. She still carried the sadness in her eyes, but she was just trying to move on.

We had little to no relationship outside of me staying at the house with the puppy when I would come home. We did not talk weekly. We really only spoke when I would come home. Occasionally she would make some meals for me when I would go back to DC, but she was very out of touch with my life. Being engaged did bring us closer together, not for wedding planning, but because my fiancés family accepted her as well. They always invited her to family events whether it was just an outing or a holiday. Our relationship was improving, but I did not have that close mother-daughter relationship my friends had with their mothers, especially when planning a wedding. I was just glad we did not fight. We rarely spoke about anything related to the family, because that always led to an argument. It felt like a friendship to me. I did not expect much more.

Later on that 4th of July night, Noah called me. He sounded a little drunk and stated he wanted me to come pick him up. My fiancé and I went and picked him up and as we were driving, Noah asked to see mom. I was shocked. I had kept Noah a secret for months and I knew Ethan was living at home. If I showed up with Noah, I was afraid Ethan would hurt Noah or me. I called my mom and I asked where Ethan was. She said he was out. I found out he was at Archie's. I told my mom I was coming over and I needed her to be outside on the back deck in 5 minutes. She asked me why and I told her to just trust me. As I pulled down the street I made sure that my brother's car was not there. I pulled up and my fiancé and I helped Noah out of the car. He needed assistance due to his leg injury. As he was able to move on his own, I walked up to the back door. My mom walked out. She looked up and her eyes teared up as she said his name. Noah replied with "Mommy." My mom slowly walked towards him and they hugged. At this point, I told them they only had a few minutes, as I was worried about Ethan coming back. I paced at the end of the driveway, watching for Ethan's car. My mother and Noah chatted but I have no idea what they said. I told my mother I would bring them together again but that we needed to go for now. For the first time in 12 years, my mom smiled, and showed emotion. I knew she was happy to see Noah. Noah got back in the car and I took him back to the rehab center.

Later that night I had to go home and explain everything to my mom. She was not mad surprisingly, but just as I had hoped, she was happy. She wanted to talk to him more and wanted to see him again. I told her that for now, Noah asked me to mediate the visits and to have them go through me when I was home. She was not crazy about that but agreed to it. We agreed not to tell Ethan yet, as we were both afraid for how he would act.

Eventually the visits transitioned from me being present handling all communications between Noah and my mom to Noah being able to directly contact my mother. That winter Noah came over for Christmas. Noah got me a Christmas present for the first time in over a decade, and I was overjoyed when I already was used to not getting gifts, but to get one from Noah after so many years, I was touched.

By this point, Ethan had learned that Noah was coming around and was in contact with my mother and I. Ethan hated Noah and blamed Noah for everything in our lives that went wrong. Ethan then decided that he would not come over for Christmas if Noah was there and Noah returned with the same sentiment. Neither of them wanted to be around each other. Ethan showed more anger towards me for being the reason Noah was back around. It continued like this for the holidays and birthdays.

One Christmas, Noah drank a lot of alcohol, and the conversation of the abuse that occurred when we were kids came up. I brought up the day Noah attacked me and my mom went into denial about it. Then Noah walked my mom through it. She maintained she did not believe it happened. That hurt me inside, but I think it was her way of blocking bad things out so she could just live.

I soon brought up the topic of my wedding. I asked if Ethan would come if Noah was there and vice versa. They both agreed they would not attend if the other were in attendance. That caused a lot of anxiety for me when I was working on the invitations to my wedding. It added to the already stressful moments of trying to get a hold of my "dad" to see if he would be in attendance.

2011 became a very trying year for me. Full of ups and downs. I attended 11 weeks at the FBI Academy's Intelligence Analyst training, and graduated in March 2011. I was transferred to the Philadelphia Division of the FBI. I applied for the transfer because I was struggling financially and I wanted to be closer to my fiancé. I moved to Philadelphia in May 2011 and lived in northern Pennsylvania. It was hard picking up a life I just started in DC with new friends and starting over again, but I think it was a good decision for me. This allowed me to have an easier commute back to Connecticut and provided a lower cost of living.

As I continued to have a lot of time to myself I began to process everything from my childhood as well as what was going on with Noah. I was able to do a lot of processing without the stress of my childhood home around me. I was able to start to reflect and look back at my life without having the people who were involved in it around me constantly. This is where I started to come to some major realizations about my life. I decided I needed to start putting myself first, and I needed to put my life back together. I knew I was still very self-conscious and was still coming off a depression and period of emotional abuse. The first major thing I did: I called my wedding off.

I realized that my fiancé was not ready to move and was not making the effort to come see me in the year we had been maintaining a distance relationship. I had made it clear that I wanted to be an FBI Agent and that would require me to move wherever the FBI wanted me to go. They call it the "needs of the Bureau." I was not going to give up my dream for anyone. I knew I had worked too hard for where I was in my life and I could not give it up. He and I both talked it out on New Years Eve of 2011. We decided it would be best if we split up. We had the support of his father and in the end we both knew it would be best. I did not want him to resent me for making him leave his family for my career, and I did not want to resent him if I chose to give up my dream. This decision was very difficult as I loved this man very much. However, I loved him to the point that his happiness meant more to me even if it meant I was not that person to provide it. We maintained a friendship for as long as we could but after a few years, we decided it was just too hard. Since then he has married and has a child, and I could not be happier for him. I know it was the right decision, as I continued on in the path of my dream and he continued on to live his life in Connecticut.

Part of rebuilding my self worth and confidence meant processing everything but also not being afraid to confront my past and to forgive. It meant I needed to surround myself with people that support me and could also understand my down moments and help me through them. It meant I needed to open up from the mask of happiness I put on all the time at work and be vulnerable, which was something that was a slow process for me.

The FBI brought me a lot of blessings. Not only did I love my job as an intelligence analyst, but I was introduced to two people along my way to my dream of being a Special Agent. The people helped me open up all over again.

I have a tattoo on my inner right forearm of the Zia Sun Sign symbol from the New Mexico state flag with an arrow going through it. I got this tattoo in the fall of 2017 while I was in New Mexico. This tattoo was for Troy and his family, who live in New Mexico. I met Troy at Analyst training in January 2011. During introductions in our class, I stated I was an avid basketball player. Troy too stated he loved playing basketball. He, to this day, said he could not believe I played basketball and could hold my own against the guys.

A week or two later, Troy, our friend Harold and I found ourselves scrimmaging on the basketball court after hours. I started raining three pointers on him and he realized I could hang. I became the secret weapon and we never lost a game against the teams we played. Troy and I began to bond over football and basketball. We lived off base for training so many times I would ride in with Troy and Harold to class. We were like the three amigos. Troy had a daughter a few years younger than I and he told me I reminded him of her. Her name is Taylor.

One day, Troy and I were hanging out and I was having a down moment. I was struggling with the relationship back home in Connecticut and dealing with the dynamics of Noah's view of my life. This was the first time I realized that if people wanted to understand why I get upset about things, they needed to know the background, and I needed to be OK with talking about it. I told Troy about my upbringing, and to my surprise we related on some things. He was a kind man with a warm heart and helped me talk out my feelings. He was like a dad to me, and I had missed that camaraderie. I always wanted a dad to talk about my relationships with, let alone my other battles. I never knew what a man was supposed to treat me like and he was helpful in guiding me on the correct trains of thought. During those 11 weeks of training, we became inseparable.

After training, he was assigned to the Albuquerque Division and he headed west. But we never lost touch. I try to go out there yearly and I speak to him regularly. I eventually met his daughter and she is like a sister to me. We try to coordinate when we fly in to see Troy so we can hang out together. His family has welcomed me in and although they are so far away, they feel like close family. Since 2011, Troy has helped me through the heartache and processing of a lot of my childhood and I am forever grateful for him and his family.

I have another tattoo on my inner right forearm. It's a compass. The compass is a replica of a coin I was given in September 2014 from a Special Agent of the FBI Philadelphia Division, who became a strong role model to me. His name was Al. He was one of the friendliest people in the office and everyone loved him. In 2012, I was asked to work a case with him on the Counterterrorism side and it required him and I to travel out to Harrisburg for meetings from Philadelphia. The car ride was over two hours long, so within those two hours we got to know each other. On one of the rides he politely asked me "what's your deal M?" I remember laughing and asking him what he meant by that. He continued on. He told me how I was such a good person, smart and very involved around the office. He knew I wanted to be a Special Agent as well. He asked me again, "What's your deal?" He was the second person I told in the FBI about my past. I was able to call Troy for advice or talk things through, but it helped having someone who was in the same geographical area that I could trust. Al kept an eye on me and was always there when I came back from trips to Connecticut that did not go so well. To this day he continues to be a mentor and inspiration to me.

When I applied to a Special Agent at 23 years old, Al was by my side helping me train at the track. He was there giving me advice on my career decisions to help set me up for success. He stood by me when I had to battle with the Human Resource department about my mental health history as a teenager. When I applied to become a Special Agent, because I would have to carry a gun full time, my short history with suicide was scrutinized in appropriate fashion. I had already passed all of the stages of the application process, including the panel interview. An interview many older Agents thought I would not pass, being only the minimum age for an Agent. Most Agent applicants are in their second career when they apply and are around age 30. After months of back and forth with the Human Resources division and scrutiny of my mental health record and work history, I was finally cleared for appointment as a Special Agent. In September 2014, the weekend of mother's birthday, I reported to the FBI Academy again to begin training as a Special Agent for 22 weeks. Al gave me the coin that is on my inner right forearm when I left for the academy.

Graduation day was bittersweet. It was one of the biggest days of my life to date. This time, I was graduating as a Special Agent. At this time, my brother Ethan and I had sat down and decided to give our relationship a go, so my mother, Ethan and Ethan's girlfriend joined Al and other family and friends for my graduation. Ashley, the girl from the first day of work was there too. She and I had grown very close after meeting at a Christmas party back in 2010. We were like "sisters from another mister" as they called it. After the ceremony, I was ecstatic to have achieved my life long dream, and I had planned a group lunch so we could all hang out before splitting up. Much to my surprise, since things seemed to be going well, I got a call from my friend Maria who let me know my mother was leaving. I quickly rushed downstairs to the lobby of the FBI academy to find my mother and brother, and his girlfriend getting ready to leave. Ethan was my mother's ride back to Connecticut and Ethan did not want to stay for the lunch because of the traffic. I felt like I was slapped across the face. I did not want to make a scene, but I was hurt. I expressed my feelings in a professional way and off they went. At lunch, explaining my family did not want to be there because of traffic was embarrassing. But I knew it was because Ethan hated it. I knew he hated being around my accomplishments since he always had. When I got home that weekend, I told my mom that she was the mother and he was the son and that it was not fair. And that I was hurt by them leaving. She teared up, and I hated seeing her upset. So I hugged her and said it's OK. But to this day, it still hurts me.

I graduated from the academy and was assigned to the New York Field Office as my first office as an Agent. I was placed on a violent crime squad, a very active squad that is intertwined with the NYPD. Every time I go through a door for a warrant, I always find myself trying to make a good impression on the kid who is there watching everything happen to their family. I remember the New Haven officer who gave me hope at a time of turmoil in my life and I wanted to give it back.

As a new Agent, once on your squad, you get assigned a training Agent. I was fortunate enough to be assigned a training Agent whom I now see like a brother. He is a former lawyer, and had been an agent for about 6 years when I met him. He knew how to run operations in the field, and everything legal. We clicked. He was slightly unorganized and I was a super organized crazy person. I hated not having things clean and in place because of the condition of my house growing up. So we were a good ying and yang. Our sense of humor aligned and I eventually confided with him on my past during a trip down south to catch a fugitive. He has been there for me as a coworker and as a friend the last 4 years. I am forever grateful to him as he inspires me daily not only to be a better Agent, but to work on things about myself. He has seen me take things personally, because that's what I always did, I always carried the weight, and he has been able to slowly get me to separate work and criticism and personal growth. That is a lesson I needed and will no doubt help me as I continue to progress within the FBI. I am hoping he will stand beside me on my wedding day and give a speech as a brother would for his kid sister, likely to embarrass me but it will be well deserved.

As for the FBI? I love it. I have been fortunate to travel the world overseas to Africa multiple times with the Evidence Response Team, respond to mass shooting scenes and bomb scenes in New York and other areas of the United States. I have had the opportunity to learn from the most senior and well-respected Agents I have ever met. I am still a young agent with a lot of career left to go, but I want to continue to learn and grow from those who are well respected within the organization, that is full of heart and passion. I love knowing that every day is different and every person I meet has a different amazing story as to why they serve with the FBI. I am fortunate that I will get to be in the FBI for well over 30 years if all goes accordingly, and I hope to take lessons from those before me so I can be a better person and a better agent.

Being an FBI Agent was a dream come true. A dream some college professors said is rare for someone under the age of 30. I was not going to let anything stop me.

Since being in New York, I have been able to work on my relationship with my mother from a distance and it's improving every day. There are days she now will call me just to check up on me and that took years to achieve. I could not have been where I am in life in 2018 mentally and emotionally without the help of Joey, Troy, Al, Kim, my training Agent, all of the teachers from elementary school, the support of the professors in the criminal justice program at the University, my victim advocate, and all the other people I have been blessed to have in my life.

Living My Dream

"Overcome", in Egyptian Hieroglyphics is tattooed on my inner left bicep. I got this tattoo after coming back from a study abroad from Egypt. It represented my love and respect to an ancient culture which I loved studying as well as convey the message of my life, overcoming obstacles. The ancient Egyptians defied natural barriers and built the amazing pyramids. I was able to overcome my obstacles and not go down a path many thought I would.

"I am the hero of my story, I don't need to be saved." These are song lyrics from a song by Regina Spektor tattooed on my inner right bicep, with a heartbeat line going between the two lines of text. This tattoo represents not being a victim, but seeing yourself as a survivor. It's my message of feeling as if I had to be the hero at times to get to where I was, I could not wait for someone to save me.

As I previously stated, 2011 was a turning point for me. I decided to put myself first. I learned a lot of tricks to help me not sink back into a depression as a young adult, after I called my engagement off. I rarely consumed alcohol until my late twenties. I started going to therapy as a young adult as I was processing my feelings and past. I picked apart every incident from start to finish and tried to see it through everyone's eyes in the family. I then let it go after I felt it was explained to me in a way I could accept it.

Trust was very hard for me most of my life. I never wanted to get hurt or abandoned, but eventually I had to trust people and not hold other's actions against a new person's intentions. I learned to open up to those I trusted. I learned how to forgive. That was my biggest and hardest lesson- forgiving people who hurt me. I can't say it did not scare me to forgive and open myself to vulnerability with that person again, but I always believed you could have one mistake with me, and if we could work it out, then I could forgive.

I began to study psychology on the side. Not only because I was interested in it for my line of work, but also because I thought it may help me in my path to forgiveness. I decided before I could go back to Connecticut and engage with my brothers and mother, I needed to try and understand their perspectives before I try and talk to each of them about our pasts. I read many books and watched a lot of documentaries on emotional trauma, physical trauma and adoption. Then I applied what I learned to each of my family members.

I looked at Ethan's upbringing and forgave him for the anger he felt deep inside, and for all the times he hit me and said mean things. He did not know how to handle his anger. And he was doing the best with what he had. He had no male role model showing him the way. He was bullied, and he was the oldest. He did what he knew.

Then I went on to analyze Noah's history. The little I knew about it at least. A woman manipulated him during a time of transition in his life. And he was vulnerable. He lived with my brother Ethan and I do not know what happened to him in that room, but I knew Noah and Ethan were not allies. I forgave Noah for leaving for what he thought was a better situation. He never had control over how my mother reacted when he left. And he did not see the manipulation Barbara had on him when he was young.

I looked at my mom, and she took me years to forgive. The woman who was supposed to protect her children. The woman who just fell into a shell and gave up. I forgave her, but it was not until 2014, when I overcame my anger towards her. Her childhood wasn't easy, and she lost her mom and sister young. My grandfather was not kind to her. She lived under the strict hand of my grandfather. She decided to adopt three children as a full time teacher. And she did a great job balancing both when she was healthy. Being a single parent with three kids is an amazing feat. And then she was struck with the cancer diagnosis, losing a son, and grief all at once. She lost some good friends and had others manipulated. She fell into a depression, but I can't blame her. She had been through so much, I just think she could not take anymore. I had to just let everything go that happened to my family and I after her illness. I could not be angry at the person who brought me here as an orphan, and gave me a chance at life. I could only forgive her and try to move on. And that's what I did. I had to get the anger out. I screamed at my mother many times when I first started processing things from the past. I just wanted her to admit she knew what happened to me as a child, or for her to see that I felt a lot of pain. I realized she too had blocked out a lot of things. Screaming about all of the bad things that happened under her watch was of no use for the time we had left together as mother and daughter. I had to redirect that anger. I put that into my workouts and my passion for helping others.

I also get asked how I deal with everything I went through. My response is I dealt with everything the same as anyone would deal with challenges in their life. Just because I had a lot of things happen to me, doesn't make my journey any less tough than someone else's. To each his own. For me, I listen to music and lyrics. That's what helped me through everything when I was young and into my adulthood. Lyrics that touched me and helped me express my feelings. I used to listen to crazy dark music from Good Charlotte, Linkin Park and Trapt as a teenager. These talented artists communicated the pain I felt through lyrics and melodies. When I began to work on my emotions and looked at things positively, I transitioned to Country music. To this day I sing Country music because it keeps me, smiling and upbeat.

I try my best to help children in foster care, and/or those with a history of suicide, depression, or sexual assault. Working with children with a similar background helps keep me in check of my emotions. It allows me to continue to be aware of what I have been through and to use those experiences to help others. I feel like I can truly connect with those children. Numerous times at work, I have shared my experiences with children victims in an effort to help them open up. I realized sometimes all they needed was someone who understands their story, to get them to trust a new person. I never want a child to feel alone or grow up thinking they cannot be anything they want to be. I also never want the people who I care about to not feel my love. Everyone deserves love. One of the most common comments I get when people learn my story is it's amazing how I decided to choose the path I did in life, rather than that of drugs and alcohol. It's because along the way, I had good role models, and people who believed in me, and sometimes that's all you need, as cheesy as it sounds. That's what I try to be- a person who is just there to help and understand or even relate to, and show that you CAN beat stereotypes, you just need to have that support. I didn't want to be a stereotype, I wanted to achieve my dreams and be happy.

In life you are always on a mission to find your true happiness, and that's all I have strived for my whole life—to find my true north in life—where I am destined to be. The obstacles that I've faced were all part of that journey for better or for worse. Because of those obstacles, I am prepared for whatever the future brings me in love and in life. Frequently, people judge other people by the way they look or how much money they make or their jobs. In reality, you never know what kind of battle a person has experienced. Most people who meet me would never have an inkling into my past—and I am OK with that. But it has taught me to always get to know someone for the person they are, not who they appear to be or on the judgments of someone else.

I have my days when I am down, and I miss my brother Noah, wish that my family was closer emotionally or days that I battle with my depression. But then I remember, I control what my true north is and where it is. I WILL find it and that's all that matters. I accept people's "baggage" because I don't see it as baggage. I see it as wounds and scars that have made you the person I want to know and it is part of your story. That's the story I want to know. People can judge me and think what they want, but I will never be untrue to myself, and my happiness, that's the lesson I have learned through all of this. I love deeply because I know what it feels like to not be loved, sometimes I get hurt because of it, but I am just happy I can feel love again, and know what it feels like to give love. I now find myself sometimes crying over the craziest stuff during movies because I can relate in some way. And I am so embarrassed I cry but then I remember when I was not able to cry. This is real life. This is emotion. And I am alive.

Finding Gracie

"Janaki" is tattooed in Arabic, on my right ribcage. Janaki is the birth name given to me at the orphanage in India. Recently, a young Indian woman in the FBI told me about the story of my birth name and who Janaki was in Indian culture. She was a beautiful princess who was adopted by Lord Rama at a young age and then kidnapped later in life. She was eventually rescued.

The distressed Peacock feather. This feather is on my left forearm. It represents the national bird of India. It is distressed at the bottom representing my childhood but at the top of the feather, it is beautiful and re-built, representing me as woman today.

Hindi writing wrapping around my left forearm, a famous quote from the late Gandhi "My life is my message." Although there is a lot of discussion about the actions of Gandhi, the quote is powerful to me, as it's exactly how I feel about my life. I live my life with a passion to help others and show love to all I encounter, whether it is through sharing my story or protecting this country.

The Broadway Lion King is tattooed on the rear of my left arm, just above my elbow. It has multiple meanings. First and foremost, the Lion King has been my favorite movie since I was a child. I am not sure why, but I was intrigued by the story and when I moved to New York City and saw the Broadway show, it solidified my love for the story. Secondly, I chose the Lion because of what the animal itself represents. A Lion represents courage. Lastly, in February 2016, the movie LION came out. It was the story of a young Indian boy named Saroo who gets lost on a train in India and eventually becomes an orphan. He then is adopted by an Australian family and as an adult makes his journey back to India in search of the family he left behind years ago.

Since I was a child, I had always wondered what my birth parents looked like, where I would have grown up, or what the place was like that I was born in. As I grew up, I distanced myself from the traditional Indian culture, trying to avoid being more different that I already was on the outside. I also did not understand the culture so I was not ready to embrace or pretend I was something I was not. As I grew older, and I started to find my love for traveling the world, I juggled the idea of going back to India. Not to per se, "find" my parents, but I wanted to see India, I wanted to feel India through the smells, sights and people. In the fall of 2015 I decided to do the new DNA kits that were coming out just to see if I had any siblings or parents that were in the database. This was my first step towards getting to India. The results came back but just many distance cousins and confirmation I was indeed South Asian and Indian. Then the movie LION came out. And I felt so connected to that story just through the preview that I wanted to see it.

It was January 2016 and I was home recovering from a double jaw surgery for my severe overbite. When I was well enough and my swelling had gone down enough that I figured I would not get stared at in public, I bought a ticket to the move just before it went out of theaters. I went back to the theater I worked at in my hometown on a Tuesday afternoon. I walked into the theater and it was quite barren as expected. A few older women and I occupied the theater. As the movie played, I could not help but tear up multiple times. I am sure the women thought I was insane with the sobbing I was holding back at times. Some moments I remember really relating to were the scenes where Saroo is a young adult battling with loving his adopted family but also wanting to find his birth family. For Saroo, his story was different than mine in that he remembered his family and was lost versus being put into an orphanage voluntarily; but that battle is similar when you love your adopted parents but also want to find those back in India. I also related to the journey of growing up different and losing a brother. Again, a different circumstance but all moments I could relate to in part. This movie was the first movie I had ever truly felt understood international adoption and how a child raised in another family longs for that belonging. This is what pushed me to really decide to make the journey back to India for my 30th birthday.

As soon as I got home, I began researching all of the different things first about my place of birth. Meaning the actual place, not the country. I did not tell my mom why, but I asked her to remind me of the names of the places I was born in. She gave me the name of the nursing home and the place I was adopted from, called IMH. IMH stood for International Mission of Hope. I had always thought I was "given up" for adoption just like kids get adopted in the United States. I thought IMH was just an adoption agency. The day I decided to do some background research on IMH to help me plan my trip back to India, I learned it was not that. IMH was an orphanage. I was an orphan. Something my mother never told me. I remember reading articles about the orphanage and learning IMH was closed for alleged baby trafficking. I read article after article and wanted to learn more. I stumbled upon a Facebook group that had all IMH adoptees from around the world who posted their adoption stories and pictures for people to see. A lot of the people within the group all had a similar story to mine. Similarities such as: having little to no records from IMH available to track down birth parents and stating the records were destroyed. According to our paperwork, as infants we were considered abandoned, and most of us were assigned birthdays and birth names at the orphanage. I learned a lot about the orphanage from the Facebook group. I saw pictures of the various orphanage locations IMH operated out of. I was not sure which location I was in, but it was another question I wanted answered. I read the posts about the baby trafficking. I read stories from those who had visited India and the orphanages. I learned about the book that tracked all of our baby names and when each baby left the orphanage. There were so many things that I learned, but also many things that hit me all at once emotionally.

I remember sitting on my bed staring at my computer after a long day of research. My brain was exhausted. I did not know what to say to my mother about learning that I was an orphan or that my research just reinforced my drive to go to India. My next step was to figure out how. I knew it would be expensive, and I wanted to get the most out of the trip. I also knew I had a language barrier I had to overcome as well. I knew nothing about traveling there except what I had read online.

There was a girl who posted about a program called "TIES" so I began to research this program. In summary, the company plans and coordinates trips for children who are adopted from overseas and want to go back to their home country. They have relationships with the orphanages or adoption agencies and work with each family on the trip to plan the adoptees trip back to their country. They run trips for numerous countries including India. Included in the trip cost are hotels, most native meals, holiday celebrations if applicable, a tour guide with knowledge of the culture, historical visits to learn the history of the country, visits to orphanages, visits with children who lived on the street (in India's program), and travel to each adoptees home city and orphanage. This was perfect. It would give me the experience of the food, and a chance to learn the culture but also the ability to see Calcutta, the place I was born and my orphanage. On the trip you are accompanied by a social worker who held sessions throughout the trip to aid in the processing of the experiences. I knew this is what I wanted to do. I looked at the cost of the trip. It was manageable and to me, worth the cost to not have to worry about anything except getting to India.

Next, I needed a companion. I knew I could not go alone, and my mother does not like flying nor could she handle the trip from a health standpoint. So I called my best friend Ashley. Ashley, ironically, is the girl I met the first day of the FBI. The stunning woman with black hair and dressed like a model? Yup! She and I became the closest of friends, much like sisters and she too had a travel bug. She was one of the first people to know my story as I was processing everything when I joined the FBI and I knew she would be a great support system. I called her up and pitched the trip to her after I saw round trip airfare was affordable a year out. She asked her husband and before I knew it, we were planning the trip.

After putting our deposits down, I knew I needed to talk to my mom. I not only needed to discuss with her the realization of me being an orphan but I also needed to explain to her why I wanted to go to India. I knew, from my years of researching adoption, that she would think I was trying to find my birth parents and replace her. And I knew my answer to that fear was just this: Mom you are my mom. And no one can change that. Blood does not make a family. Regardless of who I am blood related to, you are the one who adopted me and gave me a new life in the United States, and that is exactly what I said. I then brought up that I wish she had told me I was an orphan when I was of age to understand, as yes I was hurt by the mere fact of being abandoned, but at a certain age I would have known how to process it better. She had no response to that point in my conversation as her and I were still not very close. This entire conversation about India was the most conversation we had since I was ten years old; it was a good start.

Ashley and I departed for India December 27, 2016. It wasn't of course without a good travel story. I was all packed and ready to go. I had to get some Malaria pills before traveling to India, which I had taken on work trip to Africa numerous times without issue. However, the dosage from the travel clinic was different from that of the ones I receive for deployment. I was up the entire night with an adverse reaction resulting in the ginger ale in Saltine diet. Ashley found me on a bench clutching my ginger ale and saltine diet when she arrived in France for the last leg of the journey east. It was ironic to say the least. The next day we arrived in Delhi and began the journey.

We were sure to post daily on social media about the adventures we were on and accompany the recaps with pictures. I brought a journal with me to document the journey as well. The first few days in Delhi were an adjustment. The air was thick, the weather was cold with a high of 60 degrees and the buses did not have heat early in the morning. The streets were over crowded and people, including children, were begging for food and money everywhere. We stayed in hotels that provided us the comfort we are accustomed to back in the United States. This allowed the adoptees to have decompression time from the days' activities. I was surrounded by people that all looked like me for the first time in my life. And that was the first shocker of the trip. I finally felt like I belonged. I know the citizens could tell I was not raised in India by my tattoos, clothes and language, but it was sobering to feel like I belonged. Ashley, with her vibrant red hair became a celebrity everywhere we went and was frequently asked for pictures. She asked me if it was like that for me in the U.S. and I said sometimes, especially with the common question of "where are you from?" being a common conversation for me back home.

On our trip there were about a dozen adoptees and their parents. I was the only adoptee traveling with my friend and we jokingly called Ashley my mother. There were two other adoptees who were older. Whitney was in her early twenties and another girl was my age. The social worker, named Mara, was also my age and was also from my orphanage. The rest of the adoptees were 16 and under. All of the adoptees were females on this trip. Some were adopted as infants, and others as toddlers. Some remembered their time in India and some did not want to. All of us were from different parts of India. All of the days were packed with cultural experiences, native meals, and learning about children of India.

Ashley and I developed a friendship early on with Mara and Whitney. We soon learned that Whitney was also from IMH and she and her father would be going to the Calcutta leg of the trip with us. We were the only two adoptees going as Mara had to stay in Delhi for coordination purposes. Whitney's older brother who was my age was from IMH and living in India. He had done this trip in previous years and was able to give Whitney some tips, which she shared with us.

One of the first experiences I remember was visiting one of many government run orphanages. Outside of the orphanage was a basket, similar to the one that all of the babies would arrive in from when in transit from IMH to the United States. The basket was in a small stone cubby and was a place where infants could be abandoned in, for the orphanage to take in. The basket was iconic to many of us who have only ever heard of the baskets we were carried in as infants. Inside the orphanage, we saw men working construction jobs in dress clothes and sandals, with minimal equipment as they renovated the facades of the brick buildings. The interior had a dirt courtyard with a multi-level living structure and classrooms below. We walked around and we first went up to the nursery where we saw newborn babies being cared for. I finally could understand why my mother loved the big brown eyes on an Indian baby so much. Some were premature and hooked up to tubes, which reminded me of who I think I was when I arrived in the orphanage. Others were sleeping quietly. I asked one of the women about the adoption rates in the orphanage and she stated that nearly 90 percent of the children, infant and young find a home, but what she said next both made me happy and broke my heart all at the same time. I had always said I wanted to have a child. Whether that child was adopted or I gave birth or both, I definitely considered adopting a child from India myself. I asked about the process for international adoptions and I learned that due to the baby trafficking and human trafficking epidemic in India, children could no longer be adopted by an overseas family unless the child had a severe medical condition or if the child was legally abandoned with paperwork. Very few children are legally abandoned. This small fact broke my heart, but I was also glad to see the government was taking steps towards combating the trafficking problem. We continued our tour and got to sit in on a class of young boys and girls ages 6-12. They were learning English Language along with Hindi. I loved seeing the children so happy and eager to learn. They were all well dressed and appeared comfortable. This made me happy to see the development of these orphanages.

Another experience I remember was getting used to the food. The majority of the trip we ate native Indian dishes. I had always been against trying the food as it was not Italian and that is what I liked. As I said before, my mother would take me to that India mart as a child but I never wanted anything except the mango ice cream. I made sure the food I ate was not too spicy because I am a wimp when it comes to spice, but I was presently surprised at enjoying many of the dishes. Many of them were healthy and were comprised of vegetables and grains. The curry flavors were deep and I was glad I got to learn about Indian cooking.

One of the first few nights in Delhi, we went Sari shopping. As a child, when my mother took me to the cultural camps, I would wear a Sari, which was the traditional wear for Indian women. They are wrapped around a woman and usually vibrant in color with hand beading on the more expensive ones. On a woman's wedding day, the woman traditionally wear gold and red Saris. When I was first engaged in 2010, my wedding was planned out to be a traditional American wedding with a white dress. I never understood why my mother was so angry that my dress was not red. Fast forward to the present, that view has changed. Now that I wanted to learn about my Indian culture, I decided before going to India that I wanted my Indian culture incorporated into my wedding, if I ever get married. I wanted to purchase my red and gold Sari in India. I still wanted to wear a white wedding dress and get married in the country, but I wanted to have the Sari be incorporated to show that side of my life. I purchased a hand-beaded red and gold Sari as well as a purple one to wear for the New Years Eve celebrations in India. Many of the younger adoptees had learned how to wrap Saris at the cultural camps they went to every year and they all showed Ashley and I how to wrap ours.

We visited another children's community called the SOS Children's Village in India. It was a small community with multiple homes, run by a single woman who cares for multiple orphaned children. We spent time with a little girl named Ruti and learn about her family and life at the Village.

Ruti was an 11 year old girl who loved English and hated math. She lived with four other brothers, two sisters and her mother. She was in "Sector 1". The village was comprised of five houses of four clusters in the village of children. They went to school, raised animals, learned how to live in a family setting with other children, grew gardens, performed chores and grew up together. Ruti dreamed of being an airline hostess or a social worker one day. She was very energetic, social and was very excited to learn about us. She was very curious. When Whitney and I told her we were adopted from Calcutta she replied in an excited voice and with big eyes, "TOO CUTE!" She had a caring soul with amazing dreams and amongst adversity showed the hope and ambition these children have. She was a magnifying little girl who I wish I could have adopted. Her story is inspiring.

Learning the history of India was interesting and included tours of a lot of mosques and temples. The architecture was breathtaking and was not without the stop to the infamous Taj Mahal. We saw how white marble inlays are hand made, watched large loomed rugs be loomed by hand and washed. We traveled from Delhi to Agra, learning the history of the country and in return I gained an appreciation for where I came from, but my biggest curiosity was of my home state of Calcutta.

One of the most inspirational people I met in India was Junaid. Part of the trip included a visit to Salaam Baalak City Walk. This was where we had the opportunity to meet someone who grew up on the streets of India, and hear their story as they gave us a tour of the city and explain how children grow up in the streets and survive. Junaid was taken in by Salaam Baalak and was our tour guide.

Junaid was a young man who grew up on the streets of India. He does not know his true age but he came to the Salaam Baalak City Trust when he was around six years old, making him around twenty years old on the day of the tour. He used to live in the countryside in a place called Bihar with his mother, two sisters, brother and father. His father became sick and his mother sold everything including their house to pay for the medical bills. When his father passed away, his mother began working in a stone factory. His mother became depressed. One of his sisters passed away. His other brother and sister were not doing well so he decided to come to Delhi to help provide for his family when his begging resulted in little return. He jumped a train without any permission and unbeknownst to him, he ended up in Delhi.

He immediately became lost in the crowds. He began to live out of the railway station. A man saw him crying and tried to force him into a life of crime, which involved stealing from others to get food. Junaid refused. He spoke very little Hindi since his home language was different. One night while he was crying, a young boy came and taught Junaid how to survive, fight, get food as well as who to be around. Junaid soon learned how to "rat pick". Junaid experienced the threat of human trafficking as a young boy and saw the reality of children using drugs to live. He saw children sniff gasoline to get high. He saw girls prostitute themselves out for money. Eventually a boy from Salaam Baalak City Trust met Junaid and convinced Junaid to try out the boys' shelter for a night. He was not sure at first but then ultimately decided to stay at the shelter because he missed getting an education and believed he would have died on the street. Junaid is now a young adult and still lives in Delhi. He pays rent, works part time, and provides for his family. Junaid was reunited with his family in 2014. His mother has a phone and calls him daily. His brother is in school and his sister is doing well. He planned to attend college in the United States to study Business and Tourism. This is Junaid's story and he encouraged us to share it.

As Junaid told us this story we were walking around the areas where children lived on the streets and survived off of begging and digging through the piles of trash that line the streets. He described the conditions he and other children lived in and the realities of the poverty in India. This was the moment on my trip that made me forever thankful to my mother for the gift of adopting me and giving me a chance at life. It's why I had to find a way to forgive everything because without her, I would not be where I am today.

Calcutta was the hardest part of my trip. Whitney, her father, Ashley and I set off to visit Calcutta and IMH for 2 nights and 3 days. When we landed in Calcutta, Whitney and I both looked at each other as we got off the plane, and I snapped a picture of our "first steps" back. It was a feeling I cannot describe. I could not believe I was back. Calcutta was different than Delhi. It was full of trees and monkeys and reminded me of a jungle. As we traveled to our hotel, I remembered looking out the window at every person and thinking "that could be me" or "I wonder if that's my mother or father" and at times "I wonder if I am related to any of these people?" Calcutta did not have as many people begging. Most of the mothers were saw living on the streets held their children close and raised them to live off the land. We saw families bathing along the Hooghly River behind the flower market, near the Howrah Bridge and children playing games in the mud. At times I caught myself staring at the families just observing how they grew up. I noticed that once in Calcutta, Whitney and I immediately became bonded. We had each other and we knew exactly how we both felt. We went from being pretty talkative and outgoing most of the trip to being very quiet and observant once in Calcutta. We both would be asked by Ashley and Whitney's father what we wanted to eat and we could not even think most times. Whitney and I previously discussed going to Calcutta and IMH and we both did not know what to expect. We knew we would not find our birth families. We knew our orphanage was closed. We both had pictures of us from the orphanage but that was it. We knew we were not going to see what the orphanage looked like inside like the other adoptees would. We just wanted to at least see the place we came from. That alone would provide some closure to that longing of belonging.

After visiting the flower market, our next stop was to a local home run by a woman who adopted a child from IMH. She raised her child in the United States and then moved back to India to work with children in India. She discussed some of the issues looming around IMH and the reason for its closure as well as her experience with the orphanage during the adoption of her daughter. It felt very much like a vent session and at times was uncomfortable. She asked Whitney and I what we think about our adoption and we both just wanted to know "why" and got the classic bucket list answer of "your mother loved and cared for you" and we both agreed in that we hear that all the time. That is not what we want to hear anymore and we explained we did not expect to have an answer to it either. We both had accepted that we will never know and we both teared up. We both are always frustrated when given that answer because it really shows how people do not understand that feeling of abandonment or nor feeling good enough to keep.

Whitney's family was able to track down the Auntie who cared for Whitney in the orphanage. Her name was Madoo. In the orphanage there were many "aunties" or older women who took care of the children. She was able to come to the house with her daughter and speak with us. She was, by far, the best part of this trip. She was kind and loving. She was sweet when she spoke and had a big heart. We sat and asked her questions that only she would know. We started with showing her pictures of us in the orphanage. She recognized Whitney and called her by her Indian name. She did not remember me, but she was able to give us both insight into how we lived for the short time in the orphanage. She explained that when new babies came into the orphanage, they were named either by other children or the staff. The name was usually given based off of events occurring in India or something in popular culture. The names were also sometimes related to the day of the month that they came into the orphanage. She spoke to us about playtime, what we ate for meals, how small we were and how they kept everything in a book. I wish we had more time with her. She made me feel like the women who cared for us loved us a lot.

After we sat with Madoo and talked for a while, we went out back and took pictures under the archway that read "International Mission of Hope." This archway used to hang over the gates at the orphanage and when the orphanage was closed, the woman was able to get the sign before it was thrown out and she keeps it at her house for adoptees to visit.

At this woman's house was a young man, a little older than I who worked for the woman. He too was an IMH baby, however, he was never adopted by the time of the closure of the orphanage. He was sweet and loving and was going to take us to the orphanage. We followed him in another car, and the drive there was silent. Whitney and I could not stop looking out the window as we studied the roads and the environment surrounding where we once called home. As we pulled up, it was a lot to take in. I first recognized the gate, the gate that is tattooed on my left bicep. I am not sure I was expecting much in terms of the location of the orphanage, but I think growing up in the United States I have been accustomed to the way things look. So when we pulled up and the orphanage was surrounded by run down buildings and across from a very industrial like setting that seemed sort of out of the way, I was just surprised. I just kept staring beyond the gate at the building. The IMH man was able point out and show us where the children played outside, where the kitchen was and where the nursery was. We could see the old "IMH" letters on the gate covered by the new signs for the nursing school. We could see the old welding marks for that once secured the sign we saw at the woman's home earlier that day. We stood there for about 15 minutes. We took some pictures. And felt the goosebumps. Finally I could put an image, and smells to the place I last called home. I imagined myself being walked out of the gates in a basket with my basket buddy. I was glad I came but I couldn't speak these words.

We visited the previous locations of IMH which were operated before Whitney and I were born. Then we headed back to the hotel.

The day we left Calcutta was tough. I was holding back tears on the plane and watched every moment until I could not see the ground anymore. The rest of the trip back with the group was tough. I just wanted to be back home. I was emotionally drained. Hearing the stories from all of the other adoptees was hard for Whitney and I. We were very happy for them all to see their roots and talk to people and experience their orphanages, but we were envious we could not or ever have that experience. Mara and I spoke a lot after being back about the orphanage and the trip back to Calcutta. We had similar feelings. And this trip was a fantastic resource to gain friends and connections of people that truly do understand how it feels to feel unloved and abandoned in a way that is hard to explain.

Going back to Calcutta and speaking with the mother and Madoo offered as much closure I think that I could ask for. I did not have expectations when I went, especially knowing that the orphanage was closed and under horrible allegations. I have met many more IMH adoptees and we all share a bond. Some have even gotten the gate tattoo similar to the one I have on my arm. This was the final chapter I needed, and I am glad I chose to go on my own terms and when I was ready. I forever feel connected with Mara and Whitney and their families as well as many other IMH adoptees who are on their journey to find their belonging.

It took me a while to write this chapter of the book, because I never took the time to sit down when I came back from India and process the trip. Not because I did not want to, but more so because the trip was full of emotions, both good and bad. Even while in India, I was very good about writing and reflecting in my journal every night, but soon I stopped because I was on emotional overload towards the end of the trip. I knew I needed to be in the correct mindset to write this chapter.

Somehow on one of my many adventures around the U.S., I finally have found the time to sit down and write about some of the experiences I had on my trip. On my trip back to Birmingham, Alabama in February 2019 was when I finally felt like I could openly process my experiences. I am not sure why it was on this trip I felt like I could sit down and share these moments, but I have my suspicions. The 12 months previous to this chapter, I spent a lot of time surrounding myself with supportive relationships both personally and professionally. I was fortunate to have the support of close friends, colleagues and loved ones who do not judge me, know my skeletons and continue to understand my journey. I do not keep those who are negative towards me in my life, but instead I surround myself with happiness and show appreciation to those who have held me up when I had low times or pushed me when I needed it. These people allow me to be me to feel free to be myself and I do not see myself as the girl with baggage anymore, but rather the woman with a journey of struggles with a story to tell.

My relationship with my mother since January 2016 has been growing and improving to the point where her and I talk much more regularly and seem to have an understanding about each other. That weight of feeling as if I had no connection with my mother is slowly being lifted. During the long process of writing this book, and especially during 2018, I made an effort to find all of those teachers and mentors I had from elementary school and on, and thank them personally. I shared my story with many of them and that made me feel like I could finally show them who I was, and tell them they had a role in saving my life and me becoming successful. Finally, I felt like I was happy. I had a support system of friends and mentors that surrounded me. I could see I was truly blessed and let go of so many hard experiences in my life. I learned from each of them, but in the end, they were all lessons that got me here today.

Endnote

My mom and I have a better relationship now, and after many deep talks, she is getting better at speaking to me without being demeaning. She has seen that I chose to come back and take care of her and let everything that hurt me, go. She taught me to be a good person at my roots and to love deeply. She saved me as an infant and gave me life, here in the U.S. Forever, I will always love her. And I will always be there for her.

Ethan and I are still working on our relationship. In 2017 he was doing a great job working on himself, and getting professional help. I saw the improvements in him but at times, he turned to alcohol as a way of therapy. I tried to offer my advice from experience, but I found it unaccepted. I gave him a chance to come back into my life, and when he explained he felt as if I was not his sister after I explained to him that I had to find friends as family as a kid, he felt I turned my back on the family. He believed I was not worthy to be his sister. He is angry at me for it, and I hope he can one day understand it. I have chosen to continue to focus on helping myself and not put all of my energy into others who hurt me. I will always try to be there for him, if we get to the point where it is healthy emotionally for us both. I worry about him, and I ask my local friends who are cops to keep me updated if something were to happen to him.

Noah stopped coming around in late 2012 and he and I severed contact. I feared he was involved with the wrong people and I could not risk my job for our relationship. It was a very hard decision. He was still processing his childhood just as I had done and I again could not be there for him the way he needed me to. It's rough not knowing if he is OK. I know my mother and I both check obituaries daily in the fear that he will turn up in one of them and we won't be there. Or that we won't be notified. I fear that one day he will be arrested and locked up because he was stuck in the system and never got the help or mentors I did.

Ethan and Noah are great people with good hearts deep down. But they need to find their own way back. I hope they do. It's hard not to feel like I should try harder for Ethan and Noah, I battle with it a lot, but I also know, I can't make everyone happy and I can only do what's best for me now.

I am happy. I rarely have deep depression episodes, which has been huge achievement for me. When things come up from my past, I am able to talk them out and not get sad. I have my hard days around holidays, still but I see I am worth it. I see I am a good person. And I will always help others if I can.

I hope to have a family one day and to share the love I have within me with another person. It's crazy because when I was a little girl, I never used to dream of my wedding day, but now that I have the ability to feel happy and be happy I do dream about that day. I am excited to share my love to others now. I have always said I learned a lot from my upbringing, but I will never let my children feel unloved. I took away good strong morals from my young age, but I want my children to have all that I could not and more.

I am so happy I put my career first as a young woman, because now I am settling in and am ready to put my family and happiness first, while still living my dream. I want everyone to know that you can do anything, you just need to find those people offering a hand along the way, and not be afraid to ask for help. I had help along the way when I needed it, it was just not giving into stereotypes that I had to dig my feet it and not let happen.

Be you and share your story. Let your life be your message and shine through your adversity. After all, you are given what you know you can handle. And believe in yourself and you will achieve your dreams.

I would like to thank everyone who helped make publishing this book a possibility.

Thank you to Photos by Ken Hadinoto for an awesome cover shoot.

Thank you to Ian Croughwell Films for all of the hard work and design on the images and cover art.

Thank you to all of my friends, mentors and teachers who reviewed my book, allowed me to share my story and/or supported me as I wrote this book. I am forever grateful to have you all in my life.

And thank you to all of the children and families I mentor, for pushing me to always be the best person I can be and helping me cope with my own battles.

Made in the USA
Columbia, SC
13 June 2022

61656071R00049